Camille's Lakou

Camille's Lakou

MARIE LÉTICÉE

*Translated from French and
Guadeloupean Kreyol
by Kevin Meehan and Marie Léticée*

Vanderbilt University Press
Nashville, Tennessee

Preface copyright by Kevin Meehan 2025.
English-language copyright by Marie Léticée and Kevin Meehan.
Published by Vanderbilt University Press, 2025.
All rights reserved.

Originally published in French as *Moun Lakou* by © Ibis Rouge Editions, 2016, Matoury, Guyane.

LIBRARY OF CONGRESS CATALOGING-IN-PUBLICATION DATA

Names: Léticée, Marie, author, translator. | Meehan, Kevin, 1962–
  translator.
Title: Camille's lakou : a novel / Marie Léticée ; translated from French
  and Guadeloupean Kreyol by Kevin Meehan and Marie Léticée.
Other titles: Moun lakou. English
Description: Nashville, Tennessee : Vanderbilt University Press, 2025. |
  Series: Global Black writers in translation ; vol. 1
Identifiers: LCCN 2024050311 (print) | LCCN 2024050312 (ebook) | ISBN
  9780826507679 (paperback) | ISBN 9780826507686 (hardcover) | ISBN
  9780826507693 (epub) | ISBN 9780826507709 (pdf)
Subjects: LCGFT: Bildungsromans. | Novels.
Classification: LCC PQ3949.3.L49 M6813 2025 (print) | LCC PQ3949.3.L49
  (ebook) | DDC [Fic]--dc23
LC record available at https://lccn.loc.gov/2024050311
LC ebook record available at https://lccn.loc.gov/2024050312

Front cover image: Mango branch (Mangifera indica L.): fruiting branch with
numbered sections of flower and seed. Chromolithograph by P. Depannemaeker,
c.1885, after B. Hoola van Nooten. Wellcome Collection, 16352i. Orange:
Oranges and Poppies, L. Prang & Co. (publisher), 1895, Louis Prang & Company
Chromolithographs, Boston Public Library, Print Department.

Pou manman mwen, Lina Léticée, on mal-fanm, menm!

To my mother, Lina Léticée, a badass woman!

*To my children, Lina and Michael, may my native Guadeloupe
take root in your American hearts!*

Contents

Translator's Preface   ix

PART 1. *Manor's Alley*   5

PART 2. *Monbruno Court*   29

A Spider's Web ✦ Une toile d'araignée   33

Vegetable Soup ✦ Soupe aux légumes   37

Saturday Is Coming for Every Little Pig in
the Country ✦ Tout ti kochon dan bwa, yo tout
tini sanmdi a yo   48

Twist My Head, Make Me Cry! ✦ Touné tèt'ay, i ka pléré!   51

Fetching Water ✦ Shayé d'lo   57

Mosquitos Don't Wanna Hear You Tell Them
They're Skinny ✦ Marengwen pa vlé tann di i mèg   59

Grab a Gadasammy! ✦ Prengadassamy!   61

Frébault Street ✦ Lari Frébault   64

"Those People . . ." ✦ Sé kalité moun la sa!   72

How You Doing, Baby Girl? ✦ Ka'a sa pitit a manman?   80

Catholic Church ✦ L'église catholique   88

My Crab Hole ✦ Mon trou à crab   101

Normal School ✦ L'école normale   104

CONCLUSION. *Manor's Alley*   125

Translator's Preface

Kevin Meehan

MARIE LÉTICÉE IS the pen name of the multimedia, multilingual Guadeloupean writer and educator Akosua Fadhili Afrika. Her first novel, *Moun Lakou*, was published by Ibis Rouge Éditions, a French Guyanese press, in 2016. A sequel, *Du Haut de L'Autre Bord*, appeared in 2020 and charts the further development of characters introduced in *Moun Lakou*. Both novels are now distributed by Orphie Éditions, which acquired Ibis Rouge in 2021, and a third volume is in progress. Léticée is also the author of a full-length spoken word recording of original poems in three languages titled *Triangular Poetry / Poésie triangulaire / Poweyzi an tryang* (Sugar City Music, 2017). As a scholar, she has published *Education, Assimilation and Identity: The Literary Journey of the French Caribbean* (Caribbean Studies Press, 2009), and shorter essays, interviews, and translations.

PLOT AND STRUCTURE

Moun Lakou, translated here as *Camille's Lakou*, tells the story of Camille, a young Caribbean girl living with her single-parent mother on the fringes of 1960s Pointe-à-Pitre, Guadeloupe. The author explores neocolonial culture clash and identity conflict themes that will be familiar to readers of the Francophone Caribbean coming-of-age novel and its revisions by women writers such as Capécia, Lacrosil, Schwarz-Bart, Condé, Pineau, and others. Léticée makes it her own by fleshing out a time and place not well-represented in Guadeloupean literature. While previous bildungsromane from the writers mentioned above typically focus on rural peasant and bourgeois urban settings, *Camille's Lakou* shifts location to the lakou, depicted here as an impoverished but vibrant urban environment.[1] I explore the various regional manifestations of this milieu below in sections on "The Lakou Spectrum" and "The Guadeloupean Lakou."

Structurally, the novel emerges as an as-told-to tale of Camille's childhood framed by present-day life in Florida, where Camille now resides with her husband, Jean-Luc. The embedded tale is told by Camille to Evelyn, a twenty-something Jamaican woman who works as an assistant in Camille's successful motivational speaking and consulting business. Evelyn is a great assistant but struggling as a single mother to raise a five-year-old son who is the product of a brief liaison she had with a charismatic drummer in Guadeloupe while she had been living there as an exchange student. Camille's autobiographical reminiscence—designed perhaps to settle Evelyn's anxieties and reorient her mind to a more meditative state—is striking for its cinematic detail and strong naturalist imagery comparing human existence to the lives of crabs, pigs, ants, and to other animal, vegetable, and mineral analogues. These characterizations of the harsh economic realities of life in the city are balanced by joyous descriptions of food, music, storytelling, and other realms of cultural heritage and creativity that humanize the lakou. Against this backdrop of conflicting social forces, Léticée's narrative also reveals the questioning and resistant mind of Camille. Perhaps because she is the product of a rape, and therefore somewhat stigmatized, Camille always feels herself to be among the people of the lakou— the *moun lakou*—but not of them. This mental distance becomes increasingly profound, though, as every negative articulation of the constraining social order is followed by the narrator's refrain, "Je me demandais... (I wondered)."[2] Cumulatively, these moments create a dialectical consciousness that feels strikingly similar to the refrain of Jamaica Kincaid's narrator in *Lucy*, who repeatedly asks the people around her (and by extension her audience), "How does a person get to be that way?"[3]

THE LAKOU SPECTRUM

The centrality of the lakou as a geo-cultural space has everything to do with the particular meaning of the Kreyol word *lakou* in the original title, and the choice to retain it, untranslated, in the English title. *Lakou* readily translates to *courtyard*, or more colloquially, *yard* in English, but the location and layout for what a yard might look like and how it might function vary across a spectrum in the Caribbean region. Readers with some background in French or Kreyol terminology and the evolution of regional social forms will likely think first of Haitian reference points for the word *lakou*. In Haiti, the lakou is an important physical compound and social structure with distinct roots in rural peasant life. Scholarship on the traditional Haitian lakou stretches back more than a century. Anthropologist Greg Beckett offers a good summary of this scholarly thread, tracing the roots of the lakou to provision grounds on colonial-era plantations. After the revolution and the demise of the plantation system, these grounds became "shared family land" and having access to it meant economic as well as social prosperity. According to Beckett:

xi

CAMILLE'S LAKOU

The term lakou has a wide range of meanings, although in the simplest terms it means "courtyard." In practice, the term names both the spatial formation of the extended family compound and the social relationships that hold among coresidents. Such compounds range in size, but they include several households organized under the authority of a central "head," usually an elderly male relative. The compound also includes shared cooking areas and a garden and may also include a family cemetery. It is the site of ritual services to commemorate the Vodou lwa, and it is a key site for the economic life of the family. The lakou also includes a plot of land collectively owned and used by all members. When children are born, their incorporation into the family and the lakou is marked by the ritual burial of the placenta at the base of a fruit tree in the family yard, a rite that signifies group membership by literally merging the child's substance with the material ground that anchors social life.[4]

In short, the lakou is "both a spatial form and a social group," and viewed from the social group perspective, "it names the most meaningful relations of belonging and affect at the center of Haitian culture."[5]

At the other end of the spectrum from the rural Haitian lakou is the world of urban yards in Kingston, Jamaica. Novelist, sociologist, and educator Erna Brodber explores this Jamaican context in her sociological study *Working Paper No. 9: A Study of Yards in the City of Kingston*. Published by the Institute of Social and Economic Research at the University of the West Indies Mona, Brodber's 1975 study distinguishes broadly between government and tenant yards, and goes on to describe no less than twenty-two variations on yards and typical yard life.[6] Dating from the eighteenth century, when "Negro Yards" were built to accommodate enslaved laborers as they moved from plantations to work-for-hire jobs in the city,

xii

Translator's Preface

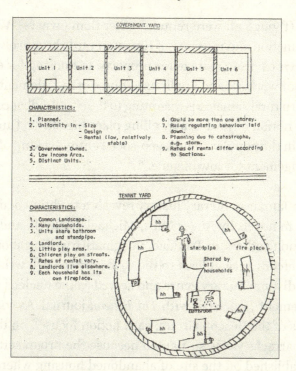

FIGURE 1. This image is reproduced with the permission of the Sir Arthur Lewis Institute of Social and Economic Studies (formerly, Institute of Social and Economic Research), The University of the West Indies, Mona, Jamaica, publisher of *Working Paper No. 9: A Study of Yards in the City of Kingston* by Ema Brodber, 1975.

Jamaican yards evolved in the post-Emancipation nineteenth century into housing for "higglers and cartmen journeying from the rural areas to sell their wares in Kingston."[7] In the twentieth century, urban transplants—and particularly single women—continued to find urban settlement options and assimilation to city life in the yards. Brodber notes a broad distinction between older tenant yards and newer government yards, with differences in spatial design such as a circular compound versus a linear array of rooms (see fig. 1), communal versus privatized single-family housing scenarios, and higher socio-economic status accorded to government yard-dwellers (though all were renters rather than owners). While the precise function and meaning of Kingston yards have evolved since the mid-1700s, from storage for property, to housing for enslaved wage-labor workers, and finally as a source of resettlement options for modern rural Jamaicans migrating to the city, Brodber concludes that "the notion of yard as a dwelling place has stayed [and] 'yard' remains in the popular mind a geo-social entity—a kind of residential arrangement for low income."[8]

While Jamaican literary history reveals a tradition of depicting the yard in novels by Roger Mais, Michael Thelwell, and Marlon James among others, in Trinidad, imaginative writing about urban yards stretches back at least to the 1930s, when such writing gave rise to a distinct literary genre and served as the nucleus of a literary movement associated with *The Beacon* journal. As codified by members of the Beacon Group, yard fiction focused on the world of the "barracks yard," so-named because the urban settlements were established on the site of abandoned housing where British troops had been billeted prior to World War I. Given that the Trinidadian yard, as described by James, Mendes, Gomes, DeBoissiere, and others, is physically located inside former British military barracks and so has an enclosed compound orientation, it combines aspects of the tenant and government yards seen in Jamaica. Like the tenant yard, there is a compound enclosure with a stone bleach in the middle and a communal toilet off to the side. Like a government yard, the barracks yard rooms are laid out in a linear row of freight boxes used originally to ship horses.[9] This account came from writer James Cummings in a 1931 essay published in *The Beacon*, in which he further describes the barracks yard as a "long line of ten by twelve boxes nailed together with a window and a door allotted to each."[10] The Trinidadian yard fiction that came out of this setting implied a methodology—writerly immersion in

Translator's Preface

yard life through participant-observation—and a style or technique blending social realism and calypsonian satire.[11]

Myriam J. A. Chancy has recently formulated the concept of "*lakou*/yard consciousness" as an inclusive framework that could highlight specific nuances along the spectrum outlined above, while linking different manifestations of the lakou together through such shared characteristics as intradiasporic cultural exchange, "a constant reconceptualization of 'home'" and the sense of belonging to "a community of like-minded folks," and a form of cultural productivity that exceeds "the constraints of national demarcations and their attendant raced realities."[12] As Chancy sums up *lakou*/yard consciousness, it emerges from a syncretic social space that "serves not as a space of assimilation but as one of *reconfiguration* in which (African) cultural antecedents are guiding principles and inspiration(s), *alongside, rather than in spite of* concepts adopted and adapted from dominant cultures within hegemonic colonial systems that remain formative whether in postcolonial (in the Americas or Europe) or postcolony (in African, after Mbembe) systems."[13] It is, moreover, a space in which "the family or kinship/cultural group can gather, rest, know itself, refuse dispersion, and pass on knowledge from one to the other, horizontally, or across time, vertically, from generation to generation."[14]

THE GUADELOUPEAN LAKOU

With Chancy's theoretical framework in mind, we can then begin to situate the world of *Camille's Lakou* within the lakou spectrum. Arguably, the milieu in Léticée's fiction resonates more closely with social patterns and creative arts from Jamaica, Trinidad, and other Anglophone islands that associate the yard with city streets rather than the rural extended-family homestead of the traditional Haitian lakou.[15] Léticée's Monbruno Court is a winding, narrow lane

xv

with multiple dwellings ranged alongside each other. People live in their own unique houses or two-room shacks (*deux-pièces cases*), though there is a massive group life formed around water stand-pipes, small stores and outdoor markets, rumshops, public toilets, and churches. Spatially, the linear appearance of housing in Monbruno Court more closely approximates how government yards are laid out in Jamaica; socially, though, the group dynamics in Léticée's Guadeloupean lakou are sufficiently strong that they evoke the more communal ethos of Kingstonian tenant yards. Interestingly, land tenure in the Guadeloupean lakou seems to include at least some level of ownership. In Jamaican and Trinidadian yards, urban dwellers rent. This small but important difference arguably sets the Guadeloupean lakou apart on the spectrum, and anticipates the comparative luxury enjoyed by the adult Camille, whose life in Manor's Alley in Florida seems on the surface at least to be quite distant from the modest circumstances of the people in Monbruno Court.[16]

LANGUAGES AND TRANSLATION CHOICES

The language spectrum in the original ranges from untranslated Kreyol in the title, chapter subheads, and numerous passages (both spoken and narrated), to standard literary French that is the vehicle for most of the novel, and occasional uses of Jamaican Patwah, Spanglish, and even standard English. This range presents a number of challenges to any translator and requires a variety of strategies for rendering Léticée's prose in English. In many instances, where the novel deploys a Kreyol phrase, I decided to inscribe the original. In the chapter subheads, I kept the Guadeloupean Kreyol and paired it with an English equivalent. With spoken passages, I tried wherever feasible to retain the original Kreyol and interweave the translation as smoothly as I could. In other places in the original,

xvi

Translator's Preface

Kreyol is dropped into a standard French passage to add what the French Guyanese writer Léon-Gontran Damas called "that Kreyol salt so rebelliously resistant to translation."[17] Such linguistic salt contributes, among other things, a measure of *mot juste* precision to descriptions of various Antillean tableaux, such as businesses in the market district of Frébault Street in downtown Pointe-à-Pitre.

The following scene describes candy vendors set up at the entrance to Frébault Street:

> Arrivées à la Pointe, nous nous retrouvions assaillies de toutes parts, de toutes sortes de bruits, d'odeurs, de couleurs aussi riches que criardes. C'était d'abord les marchandes de *dou-koune*, assises sur un tabouret de bois, au coin de la rue Frébault qui nous souhaitaient la bienvenue à coup de «*Doudou cheri . . . mwen ni sik a koko a tèt roz*», avec leurs paniers pleins de gateaux, *sik* à coco hachés et gragés, *sik* a coco à têtes roses, doucelettes bien dorées, *sik doj, sik à pistache* et bien sûr, mon préféré: dentelles de coco.

Here is my translation of that passage:

> As soon as we arrived in La Pointe, we found ourselves assaulted from all sides by every kind of noise, with smells and colors that were rich and garish at the same time. The first thing we always saw were the *doukoune* or sweet snack vendors, seated on wooden stools at the corner of Frébault Street, who welcomed us with their refrain. "*Doudou cheri . . .* Sweets, cherie, I got the coconut ball candies with the pink head." Their baskets were loaded with cakes, chopped and toasted coconut balls (including the pink-headed ones), golden *doucelettes* like caramel-fudge fondant, brown sticks of hard *sik doj* candy, sweet nougat bars with pistachio nuts, and of course my favorite: coconut lace.

xvii

CAMILLE'S LAKOU

This brief passage offers a good overview of the different translation strategies used in *Camille's Lakou*. I sometimes chose to retain a Kreyol word while adding some English to describe qualities and details conveyed only by implication in the original ("brown sticks of hard *sik doj* candy"). At other times I gave just an English equivalent, as in "sweet nougat bars with pistachio nuts" for the original "*sik à pistache*." In some instances, where Kreyol is sprinkled like Damasian salt, I put the English equivalent word or phrase in quotation marks.

One of the thorniest, stickiest, and in my mind still-unresolved issues in this translation process has been formulating a target language for Guadeloupean Kreyol. Initially, I prepared the entire manuscript using Jamaican Patwah as the target language, particularly for spoken passages. An example from another chapter gives a sense of how I tried to braid the two vernaculars in my first draft. Here, Camille makes a bold complaint to her mother about food: "*Lè ou tini soup fligé aw pou ban mwen*—when yuh tek time fe mek mi soup, why yuh cyaan gi mi some—*sé pa la pèn pan mwen'y?*" I used Jamaican Patwah to render similar moments of direct discourse whenever they appeared. Occasionally, as in the Frébault Street market scene cited above, the target was standard English, and sometimes, particularly in the chapter title subheads, I aimed for a mesolectal blending of the two, inspired by (but in no way achieving the full grace of) Marlon James's efforts to make Patwah legible to readers not fluent in the vernacular. For example, the original version of the first chapter title presented here was "Mosquito doan need you to tell him he skinny."

The author's negative reaction to my use of Jamaican Patwah to render Guadeloupean Kreyol was visceral. I should add at this point that Marie Léticée, whom I usually call "AFA" in honor of her full chosen name, Akosua Fadhili Afrika, is one of my oldest and dearest friends and colleagues. For nearly three decades, we

xviii

Translator's Preface

have worked together at UCF and have shared experiences such as co-teaching, presenting research together at scholarly conferences, co-authoring publications (including translations of Haitian Indigenist poetry), collaborating on studio recordings of her spoken word poems, and doing committee trench work in the Florida state university system. Our families have socialized countless times and bonded over food, music, gardening, and politics. The strength of this collegial relationship was the foundation for my being able to complete the translation while we were separated for nearly two years during the pandemic.

Our close relationship also set the stage for some heated polemical exchanges when we finally reconnected in December 2022 to discuss next steps for the translation; our relationship also made me, I would say, particularly vulnerable to receiving and ultimately conceding to her arguments against using Jamaican Patwah. According to Marie, Patwah diluted the impact of Kreyol by offering a form of mediation that distracted from the strong confrontation between French and Kreyol in the original, where there is, indeed, no translation of italicized vernacular passages. "That's not my Kreyol, and my Kreyol does not need to be interpreted," is one of her pronouncements that stands out in my mind. I think I had ten or twelve levels of counterargument ready to go, including the importance of fostering South-South dialogue and regional linkages in vernacular languages, the highly advanced tradition spanning generations of Jamaican writers who have developed Patwah as a literary language, the presence of a primary Jamaican character and the use of Patwah in the margins of the original, and above all the mission of translation. "How can I leave the Kreyol untranslated in a translation?" I asked. "Let the readers pick up a dictionary!" was Marie's polemical response. Adding to this friction from my side was the fact that my Patwah renderings were endorsed in peer review reports from two different journals, and one excerpt was even selected for a literary

xix

translation prize. For every counterargument, though, Marie had a powerful rebuttal, and she challenged me to consider the possibility that my translation would reinforce stereotyped perceptions by outsiders who frequently assume all Caribbeans are Jamaican until proven otherwise. She also made me think long and hard about how a "white savior complex" might be lurking behind the urge to promote *my* version of South-South dialogue.[18]

As this debate reverberated in my own thoughts and feelings, I found myself taking refuge in the idea of translation as an act of "abusive fidelity," a phrase coined initially by Phillip Lewis but elaborated upon by Lawrence Venuti in his essay on translating Derrida on translation.[19] *Yardies*, the title of the first version of my translation, exemplified abusive fidelity as defined by Lewis, that is, as translating that "values experimentation, tampers with usage, seeks to match the polyvalences of and plurivocalities or expressive stresses of the original by producing its own."[20] What I had not counted on, but what Marie forced me to see, is how the same version that might "abuse" monolingual English by interweaving Gwada Kreyol and Jamaican Patwah could also turn out to be abusive of the author's own sensibility. Given my relationship with her—one that few translators would experience with the author an original text—I had to face a reckoning with her critique. Forced to choose between my own ego seductions (a clever braiding of Kreyol and Patwah, a progressive argument for South-South dialogue, a literary translation prize), and Marie's insistence on what Glissant termed "le droit á l'opacité," (the right to opacity) I agreed to change the title from *Yardies* to *Camille's Lakou*.[21]

In making this revision, I opted for a fidelity to the original text of *Moun Lakou* that was, I think, less abusive to Marie's cultural politics but that now ran the risk of being equally or more abusive to English readers. What to do? Though I was persuaded by the author's argument to suppress Jamaican Patwah—except where it

Translator's Preface

appeared in the original—I found it impossible to simply abandon the work of translation and leave Guadeloupean Kreyol untranslated. As is evident from the Frébault Street passage cited above, while Gwada Kreyol remains inscribed in the translation, and typically appears in italics as in the original, it has been glossed in various ways with standard English equivalents or explanatory additions.

In one important instance, though, I chose to neither translate nor italicize the pivotal Kreyol keyword—lakou—beginning with the revised title. Originally billed as *Yardies*, which of course played off the Patwah word for denizens of the lakou or yard, the updated version of *Camille's Lakou* performs its own abusive fidelity. On the one hand, by changing *Moun Lakou* to *Camille's Lakou*, the English title mutes some of the collective emphasis felt in the original (*moun* means "people" in Kreyol), and refocuses the reader to expect a more individualistic narrative in the bildungsroman tradition. Whether or not the body of the novel does indeed express an individualistic versus communal ethos (I would say it honors both communalism and individuality), this title is a good example of how translation can lead to assimilation, domestication, and "an erasure of the foreignness of the foreign text by rewriting it in the terms of the receiving language and culture."[22] On the other hand, by retaining the word *lakou*, the translation forces English readers to learn this word and encounter it on its own terms (pick up a dictionary, or read this translator's commentary). By leaving it untranslated and unitalicized in the body of the novel, abusive fidelity has now gone so far as to deform and reform English language itself by embedding the Kreyol word into English, challenging readers to accept it directly (without mediation from Jamaican Patwah), and ultimately normalizing it as a part of a reconstructed, polylingual English. This is a very different translation strategy than the original conception, but my hope is that it results in a more globalectic expression of language politics, defined by Ngugi wa Thiong'o in the

xxi

following way: "There are two ways by which different languages and cultures can relate to one another: as hierarchies of unequal power relationships (the imperial way) or as a network of equal give-and-take (the democratic way). . . . The globalectic world view looks at nature, society, thought, not as a hierarchy of power relations—the current and dominant view—but as a network of give-and-take."[23] While English often takes away from the impact of *Moun Lakou* by suppressing the charged juxtapositions of French versus untranslated Gwada Kreyol in the original, hopefully the retention of the word *lakou* and the effort to mainstream it in the English translation helps to reverse the flow and reveal English in the act of receiving the original language and morphing in response to it.

I see the original novel as directed primarily to a multilingual readership that could decode all the languages and registers of meaning in the novel with ease. I have tried to convey all the thematic and psychological content of *Moun Lakou* while preserving enough traces of the Kreyol spectrum to make this beautiful rendering of the Guadeloupean lakou intelligible to all English-language readers. I would conclude by reiterating that none of this translation work would have been possible without constant input from the author, particularly regarding passages in Guadeloupean Kreyol that verge on untranslatable but whose piquant and nuanced view of Caribbean life is the source of intense poetic and intellectual pleasure. In the end, the length and intensity of our dialogue about the art and politics of translation in *Camille's Lakou* led Marie and me to a mutual realization that this is a co-translated work, one that we happily and appropriately present to readers under both our names.

Notes

Earlier versions of this "Translator's Preface" and portions of the novel translation appeared previously in *The Hopkins Review* 16, no. 1 (2023)

Translator's Preface

and *Small Axe*, no. 75 (2024). In thinking about the genesis of this expanded version, I would like to express thanks to my colleague and friend Fayeza Hasanat for talking through extremely complex questions of translation theory and practice with me, and for sharing Lawrence Venuti's translation of Derrida on translation, as well her own writing on the translation process. I am also extremely grateful to two anonymous readers who reviewed an excerpt of this manuscript for *Small Axe*. Both readers offered insightful, granular comments that led to important changes in the body of the text and this preface.

1. Comparable fiction by Haitian women writers such as Marie-Thérèse Colimon-Hall, Marie Chauvet, Edwidge Danticat, and others offers a view of poor urban settings, and Chauvet explores bourgeois life outside the Port-au-Prince metropolis. Male authors of Caribbean novels in French and Kreyol, such as *Compère Général Soleil* by Jacques Stephen Alexis or *Texaco* by Patrick Chamoiseau, also treat a broad spectrum of classes in the Caribbean city, but with the political economic framework presented in *Moun Lakou*, Léticée occupies a unique niche among women writers from Guadeloupe and Martinique.

2. Marie Léticée, *Moun Lakou* (Matoury, Guyane: Ibis Rouge, 2016), 47.

3. Jamacia Kincaid, *Lucy* (New York: Farrar, Straus and Giroux, 1990), 21.

4. Greg Beckett, *There Is No More Haiti: Between Life and Death in Port-au-Prince* (Oakland, CA: University of California Press, 2020), 44–45. See also Beckett's footnote on the century-long arc of scholarship on the lakou on page 245.

5. Beckett, *No More Haiti*, 45–46.

6. Erna Brodber, *Working Paper No. 9: A Study of Yards in the City of Kingston* (Mona, Jamaica: Institute of Social and Economic Research, 1975), 2.

7. Brodber, *Working Paper No. 9*, 6–7.

8. Brodber, *Working Paper No. 9*, 9.

9. Reinhard W. Sander, *The Trinidad Awakening: West Indian Literature of the Nineteen-Thirties* (New York: Greenwood, 1988), 36.

10. Sander, *Trinidad Awakening*, 36.

11. Sander, *Trinidad Awakening*, 69. Sander's excellent summary analysis of yard fiction style and its legacy is worth quoting in full: "In considering the barrack-yard genre as a whole, a pattern begins to emerge. The descriptions of the life and people of the yard appear overpredictable or

xxiii

stereotyped. Chinese shopkeepers are invariably caricatured as miserly, inscrutable, opium-smoking Orientals, obeah women are always black, and mulatresses are invariably unfaithful; stones are used to bleach clothes and knives are used to cut people. However, it must be borne in mind that in the history of Trinidad society these patterns had never been previously recognized and defined creatively outside of the calypso tents. By transforming popular local biases into literary stereotypes, the barrack-yard writers were able to recreate a recognizable social milieu, which, if anything, enhanced the credibility of the handful of characters in a particular story who were given a fuller treatment, and portrayed as being capable of emotions of love, hate, trust, and guilt that the reader could recognize and identify with. In this way the barrack-yard genre was able to translate the social realism of the European tradition and the comic satire of the calypso tradition into a new, intermediary form around which an indigenous literary tradition could be built. When one bears in mind the significance of this achievement for the novelists who emerged from the Beacon group and the Trinidadian writers who followed them in later years, the unique place of the early barrack-yard stories in the history of West Indian literature can be fully appreciated."

12. Myriam J. A. Chancy, *Autochthonomies: Transnationalism, Testimonies, and Transmission in the African Diaspora* (Urbana: University of Illinois Press, 2020), 18–20.

13. Chancy, *Autochthonomies*, 19–20 (italics in original).

14. Chancy, *Autochthonomies*, 20.

15. This is not to minimize or deny the importance of urban life in Haitian society and literature. Beckett writes extensively on urban migration and its impact on reshaping the lakou. Whether or not lakou traditions have survived the transition to an urban setting in Haiti is an open question. In his account, Beckett cites with approval Michel Laguerre's ethnographic account of "urban lakous"; these settlements arguably adapt lakou social dynamics to cope with "the vagaries of the informal economy and the ad hoc and unplanned space of the city itself." Beckett, *No More Haiti*, 74. Beckett also draws attention to a significant thread among scholars and social critics who have proclaimed the "death of the lakou" as a result of urban migration (44).

16. An interesting question that deserves more analysis is whether or not the older Camille retains any aspects of the lakou in her management of

Translator's Preface

business operations and social dynamics in the gated community villa that is the main setting for the opening and closing chapters of the novel. While Manor's Alley might initially seem quite far indeed from the world of Monbruno Court, one could make the case that Camille's nurturing attitude toward Evelyn and her son reveals an enduring communal ethos rooted in the lakou. While Beckett, Laguerre, Brodber, and others have explored how lakou culture evolves when traveling from rural to urban settings in the Caribbean, what happens when the bearers of that culture exit the region as migrants to Europe, Canada, the US, or elsewhere? Is Léticée mapping a migrant or diaspora version of the lakou in the Florida sections of her novel? To think about these questions more fully, in addition to Chancy's *Autochthonomies*, see a related exploration of the "dyasporic lakou" as a key aspect of effective relief and recovery work in post-earthquake Haiti in Charlene Désir, "Diasporic Lakou: A Haitian Academic Explores Her Path to Haiti Pre- and Post-Earthquake," *Harvard Educational Review* 81, no. 2 (Summer 2011): 278–95. See also a further reflection on how Désir's work on dyasporic lakou contributes to a broad cross-cultural framework of African diasporan healing practices in Alecia Deon, "Between the Worlds of the Colonizer and the Conjure Woman," *QED: A Journal in GLBTQ Worldmaking* 6, no. 3 (2019), 143–48.

17. Léon-Gontran Damas, *Veillées noires* (Paris: Stock, 1943), 12. In the introduction to this short story collection, Damas comments metafictionally on the source of his stories in folk tales recited in evenings and into the night during his childhood and later during a mid-1930s fieldwork trip through La Guyane. He highlights the important decolonizing cultural politics of returning to these sources (particularly for Caribbean migrants located in the metropole) and characterizes the feisty linguistic style of his folkloric storyteller narrator, based on a real-life nonagenarian character Tètèche: "Tout cela m'a été donné par Tètèche, assaisoné de ce sel créole si résolument rebelle aux traductions ("All of this was given to me by Tètèche, seasoned with that Kreyol salt so rebelliously resistant to translation"; 12, my translation).

18. There is plenty of scholarship on the topic of a so-called white savior complex, most recently revolving around critiques of Jason Russell's sensationalistic 2012 video documentary on Ugandan warlord Joseph Kony and the Lord's Resistance Army, but for compelling analyses that

suggest the wide range of the critical discourse, see Yusug Jailani, "The Struggle of the Veiled Woman: 'White Savior Complex' and Rising Islamophobia Create a Two-Fold Plight," *Harvard International Review* 37, no. 2 (Winter 2016): 51–54, and Leanne Betasamosake Simpson, "Indigenous Resurgence and Co-Resistance," *Critical Ethnic Studies* 2, no. 2 (Fall, 2016): 19–34.

19. Lawrence Venuti, "Translating Derrida on Translation: Relevance and Disciplinary Resistance," *Yale Journal of Criticism* 16, no. 2 (2003): 237–62.

20. Quoted in Venuti, "Translating Derrida on Translation," 252.

21. Edouard Glissant, *Poétique de la relation* (Paris: Gallimard, 1990), 209.

22. Venuti, "Translating Derrida on Translation," 257.

23. See Ngugi wa Thiong'o, *The Language of Languages: Reflections on Translation* (London: Seagull Books, 2023), 4, 54.

Camille's Lakou

To begin with, I don't even know which language I should use to express myself. I am giving in, then, to my first instinct, which imposes French language on me, that language that I could not manage to master after Madame Fabre said to me, "But you do not know how to write, Miss Léticée . . . What does this even mean??" And yet, I have this crazy desire to push out my story like a hen lays an egg. It is there, buried inside, but it is only with great pain that it reveals itself to me. Is that story afraid to let itself be discovered? Could it be afraid that Madame Fabre was right?

part one

Manor's Alley

CAMILLE SIGHED and shook her head again, one more time. She could never believe her eyes. From the corner of her meditation garden where she was lounging around as she did every morning, she could see the long winding driveway bordered by royal palms that led up to the verandah of her house. This driveway, which reminded her of Allée Dumanoir in her native Guadeloupe, opened into a large jaw-shaped area where a circular fountain was flowing with multiple jets in the style of Versailles. At the very top there was a stone racoon, an animal that was well-known in Florida but had been chosen because it was, above all, the mascot of Guadeloupe. The racoon always brought a smile to her face and made her think of the song "Ti rakoun" by Saint-Eloi.

The fountain stood in the middle of a circular median of red brick where she and Jean-Luc liked to park their cars so that they could enter the house by the front door and not by the garage. Camille and Jean-Luc loved their entryway. The front door was massive, made of cedarwood they had imported from Lebanon after their last trip to that part of the world.

Each palm bordering the driveway was resplendent with its grey skirt, hurtling itself all the way to the top where the crown ended in a single palm front thrusting proudly into the sky. The base of each tree was enveloped in a corona of red impatiens that Camille preferred because, she said, their color signified victory. She had named the driveway Manor's Alley, and it was separated from the main road by a large gate with two doors, each of which carried the letter "C" in calligraphic letters that also formed handles. Manor's

Alley stretched like a bloated serpent up to the circular fountain and the parking area that surrounded it. Camille chose this style of fountain because it reminded her of the numerous fountains that peppered the grounds of the Palace of Versailles. Hers was done, of course, on a more modest scale appropriate to the size of their house, which was styled after an Antillean villa and surrounded by a verandah where Camille and Jean-Luc liked to sit sometimes in the evening but above all in the morning, very early, to savor their morning drink while admiring the sunrise. She was café-crème, he was lemon-ginger tea.

Camille loved that fountain. She abandoned herself to her dream that, as it always did, carried her from Guadeloupe to France and always to the same places: the castles in the Loire Valley and Versailles, Dumanoir Alley in Guadeloupe, the Traversée Road to Capesterre, and Monbruno Court jammed in there between Pointe-à-Pitre and Les Abymes. For her, these places represented everything in her that was French and Guadeloupean. For a long time, she had resisted her French heritage. She had fought against all the Louis that haunted the French history books, all the Huns and the others, the Attilas and their swords! Even Clovis and Charlemagne had not been able to convince her. And when Montesquieu proclaimed in The Spirit of the Laws, "These people we are referring to who are black from head to toe, it is almost impossible to feel sorry for them," that was the last straw! Madame Siquier had really tried to make her understand that the tone of Montesquieu's text was satirical, but that did nothing to change the fact that she felt no affinity between herself and the children of her motherland. It took years and years of reading Césaire, Glissant, and Chamoiseau, Confiant and Condé and Schwarz-Bart, and Bernabé and Pineau for her to reach the point mentally where she was today. She was who she was, but she was also all of that: France, Guadeloupe, and Senegal, yes, absolutely, Senegal!

"I see you have that smile on your face again! What is it about this time?" said the man who had had joined her with a smile on his own lips, as if he already knew where his wife's thoughts lay anchored.

Jean-Luc had again surprised her in deep contemplation and she turned her head toward him. As always, she had not heard him arrive. Camille looked at him from head to toe. His long dreadlocks were still very thick and touched throughout with streaks of grey that gave him a certain sex appeal that she had a hard time resisting. His naked torso pearled with droplets of sweat. White pants of light-weight cotton revealed legs that were still very muscular along with bare feet. Turning sixty had not changed him. He kissed her lightly on her forehead and, as always, it made her entire being shiver. He smelled like fresh vetiver, lime, and citronella. She already knew how this morning was going to end!

"No, I was thinking about St. Eloi as I was admiring our racoon," she said, smiling, resisting the desire that welled up from deep within her soul to lay a soft and moist kiss on his lips.

"Ah! Patrick!" he said, shaking his head. "That man was a prophet! Pa ni pon chantè kon Patrick—nobody can sing like Patrick! This new generation of musicians today don't produce anything but junk. They're all shitheads! Did you meditate already?" Jean-Luc had perfected the art of delivering blessings and curses in the same breath. One would never believe that he had grown up in an evangelical house and attended church every Sunday for most of his life. His mother never believed me when I told her that her son had the mouth of a truck driver. Camille shook her head and smiled like she always did, with a slightly reproachful air.

"No. Not yet. I was waiting for you. How was your run this morning?"

"Oh not bad, 9:35. I wanted to do my 10K in 9:30 per mile, but that's how it goes. It must be the champagne from last night," he said, laughing. "Come on, let's meditate together!"

Meditate?! That is not what she had on her mind right then . . . But they had the whole morning for that, she thought to herself.

The Florida climate suited them perfectly. They had built a little cabana near the edge of the garden, just alongside the lake. You got to it by crossing a small bridge with a little river flowing under it that went on to empty out into the lake. The sound of the water was a constant humming that provided background noise for their meditations. They had named the bridge Pont de la Gabarre in memory of the bridge that split their Guadeloupe in two. Moreover, they had made very sure to show a map of their island to the architect tasked with planting a meditation garden that would transport them mentally to their native Karukéra, their island of beautiful waters. Even though they owned an almost identical house in Capesterre-Belle-Eau, their Floridian home had to have a Guadeloupean soul. And the architect had succeeded!

Wrapping his arm around her waist, Jean-Luc led them toward the arbor. It was covered with a roof that seemed to be made of coconut palm fronds and it was surrounded by a sheer, almost invisible mosquito netting that kept the insects away. The furniture inside was inviting and comfortable and included several thick, very large cushions that they sat on during their meditations, as well as other Antillean-style pieces made for the outdoors. The central table was in the form of a Ka drum and held an imposing allure that demanded respect. Jean-Luc gave his wife a tender push inside the arbor and reached out his arm toward a rosewood shelf to pick up a cigarette lighter he used to light several candles that soon filled the atmosphere with the soothing odor of vanilla and cinnamon. They loved these two scents. For her, it was the vanilla erupting in the Florida sun, and for him it was cinnamon that calmed his soul and filled it with sweetness. They sat down together, each one on their own cushion. Hers was red and Jean-Luc's was black.

"Ommmmmmmm . . . ." he began, after several minutes of deep breathing.

Manor's Alley

"Ommmmmmmm . . . ." she repeated automatically. Her thoughts, however, kept landing on the feelings she had for her husband of more than thirty years. She thought about how she loved this man whom she had married very late, at the end of her twenties. She had waited for years for him to make up his mind. He was obviously in no hurry. He knew she would wait for him. Perhaps he had been hoping to find another young woman, someone more beautiful than her, someone with lighter skin and hair that was smooth and long. He had been told by several members of his family that he had to lighten the race, that this Camille seemed too rough to be at his side. On top of this all she came from the slums of Lakou Monbruno. Nothing good ever came out of a lakou! Eight years she had waited in despair! Eight years!

"Om sa . . . My attention activates my desires!" She forced herself to concentrate on her morning meditation and avoid fantasizing about her own husband. She smiled at the thought. She resumed then, "Om sa . . . Om sa . . ." and really applied herself to fix her desires on what she wanted to manifest in her own life and not solely on what she had seen lurking beneath the transparent pants of her husband. "Om sa . . ." she continued, "Om sa . . ."

They always ended their meditation time with some yoga stretches, which would explain their suppleness despite the fact that they were both in their sixties. Camille was always teasing him, reminding him that she was more athletic than he since she had already run three marathons, three triathlon sprints, and a half-Ironman! And all that in her fifties! They left the meditation arbor together, racing to see who would get to the shower first. Jean-Luc always let her win and, at the end, once they reached their immense bathroom, he caught her by the waist and pulled her toward him, all out of breath. Quite deliberately, she let herself go, winding her legs up around Jean-Luc's waist, and we understood why their bathroom had a soft divan right in the middle of it. This room was as big their kitchen, where they could receive up to fifty people comfortably. It was connected to their bedroom, which took up the entire south side of their villa. In the middle of the bathroom there was an immense jacuzzi behind which sat a comfortable lounging area that contained a large red couch, a chaise lounge reupholstered with red and black material, and a cocktail table. This table also served as a wine cooler with glass windows through which you could see three shelves that supported several bottles of wine and two bottles of champagne. In a corner of the room sat a large red and gold buddha who offered, cupped in his fat and swollen hands, an incense holder exuding a sent that filled the entire bathroom area. On the other side of the room, a large statue of the Mulâtresse Solitude in the full splendor of her pregnancy brandished a lantern that lit up the statue of Vélo hugging a Ka drum in his muscular legs. Throbbing sounds emanated from the Vélo's Ka and filled up the scented air with soft vibrations that seeped into their veins.

Almost every day, then, they showered together in that sensual atmosphere, scrubbing each other's backs, bottoms, their entire bodies, with a coconut-scented soap. He nibbled on the ends of her breasts and they would harden with pleasure until she let a long, sweet moan escape from her lips as she abandoned herself to his caresses. She felt his hardened seed finding its way, moving toward the utmost depth of her being. Then, completely wet, one inside the other, they moved together toward their bathroom sofa and let themselves go in a well-syncopated dance from which they emerged saturated with love, a true love that had taken its time to mature. A love that was now at its peak despite the fact that they were both in their sixties and already grandparents! Camille had never thought she would feel this kind of love for a man she had lived with for so many years.

"I've just received confirmation of your flight for Paris on the twenty-second of this month, and I'm about to make your hotel reservation as well. Will Jean-Luc be travelling on the same flight

Manor's Alley

with you this time or will he fly ahead of you to finalize everything regarding the event?" said the young woman outside the entrance to Camille's huge office.

"Well, thank you Evelyn for taking such good care of us. Jean-Luc is on the phone. He will discuss it with you when he's done with his call. He has to sort something out that concerns Le Club de Jazz. Do you have any news about the conference in Guadeloupe?"

"No ma'am. *Pas encore*. I guess they're taking their usual small island time," she blurted out in a single breath.

"Pardon? What did you just say?"

"Oh, nothing ma'am. I just said I'm waiting for feedback from the agency in Guadeloupe for your speaking arrangement in Sainte-Anne. Apparently, the mayor is very interested in this project and would like to involve the cities of Saint-François and Le Moule as well."

"Oh, ok. I thought I heard something else."

For several years now, Evelyn had been working for this family. For her, it was an excellent position that allowed her to raise her son, Marvel, and to travel on business from time to time for Achieve with Camille, the enterprise run by her benefactor. She loved her work and adored the Chamberlain family. She would never dare to reveal what she thought of small island people, as she called them. They always took an insanely long time to do anything, no matter what it was. You would think they worked only when they felt like it. They ended every one of the numerous phone calls she had with them with the phrase, "Tomorrow, Lord willing, I'll send you the paperwork." Apparently, the Good Lord was never willing since all of them took months and months! No . . . She would never dare to say anything like that to Mr. or Mrs. Chamberlain! They had saved her life. Not only that, they were different, those two. They loved their people and had high hopes for them. They did everything they could to share their philosophy with their compatriots in the hope

13

of showing them the way to a better life. They truly believed in all that spiritual mumbo jumbo.

Camille had finally hired this young Jamaican woman after several tries with other young and some not-so-young assistants. Actually, the way Evelyn had fallen into their arms, it was as if God himself had sent her to them. On top of that, she spoke perfect French and had mastered Kreyol to the point that it felt like she had been born and raised in one of those numerous poor neighborhoods on the island. She spoke Kreyol almost without an accent, and that gave her a big advantage over the other candidates. In fact, from the time she was a teenager, Evelyn had spent several years going back and forth between Jamaica and Guadeloupe. During her last trip there, though, her life had taken a direction she could not have foreseen. She had been bewitched by the Ka drumming of this larger-than-life Guadeloupean rasta with dreadlocks that were as wild and unruly as his relations with the many young women who chased after him. People said they were all under the spell of his disarming smile and his capacity for bonding with the drum, which he mounted, caressed, and moved with as if he were making love. He was known as a grand master of the Ka in Guadeloupe and had achieved extraordinary fame from one end of the island to the other. When he rode his Ka, which he did all day long for hours on end, the sounds he was able to unleash from the instrument reached down all the way to the bottom of your gut and took you places only your soul could understand. Charly was his name, and among the elders he had the status of a *vieux nègre* who didn't care for anything except amusing himself by playing "bodobo music" all day long. This was, of course, broken up by numerous visits from the shameless young women who lined up outside his mother's front door. At thirty years old, he still lived in his mother's house. She made his meals every day and seemed to close her eyes to the sexual habits of her only son. She always said to anyone who cared to listen: "No shoulders on my cock! *Kok an mwen pa ni zépol! Tout manman maré poul a zot!* Mother hens got to mind their chicks!" Unfortunately for Evelyn, she was one of the ones who fell under the spell of Charly's Ka.

During one of her study abroad trips to Porland, Moule, she was invited by the Moulienne Youth League to attend a cultural rite of passage that happened almost every year along Rue 14-Février-1952 in downtown Le Moule. This street, which commemorated a massacre that took place there during riots between the rich white Békés and the factory workers of Moule in 1952, represented the heart of the Moulien population. Four of their own were lost while striking for the dignity of *Gwadloup* men and women and the town was proud of them! They had not let themselves be intimidated by security squads sent from France to exterminate them for the economic protection of the Békés. Four of them were killed and fourteen wounded! Up to the present moment they remembered it still, and every February 14 the people of Moule faithfully recalled these events. To be sure, this insignificant little moment did not make its way into the history books used in schools, but the Mouliens remembered, and they told the story to their children. Moreover, the sounds that emanated from Charly's fingers seemed to channel the fights, pain, and suffering from then and now. So it was that Evelyn and Charly met through the rhythm of Kaladja ten years ago. She was only seventeen years old, newly arrived on the island with her Wolmer's School group from Kingston Parish. Wolmer's and the Louis Delgrès Professional School of Moule were cultural exchange partners, and each year a small group of five Jamaican students participated in the program and were housed with Guadeloupean families. A few Guadeloupeans chosen by the study abroad committee would select five students to participate in this cultural exchange, charged with the task of representing Guadeloupe to their brothers and sisters from Jamaica.

CAMILLE'S LAKOU

This one particular night, Charly invited the pretty young ebony-skinned woman who was staying in his mother's house. He wanted to show her his island, yes, but more than anything he was determined to possess her through the beat of his charm. She was beautiful, with a face of very smooth skin and almond-shaped eyes that pierced your soul on one side and your heart on the other. She had high cheekbones like the women of Dahomey, her figure was cut like a wasp, and her butt was high and tight, just the way he liked. She also had the haughty gait of women who believe they are beyond the reach of *vieux nègres* like him. What she had not counted on, though, was the spell of his Ka drum. Not a single woman had been able to resist him, and he knew that she would soon be his. And so he had invited her to this commemorative *lewoz* parade that was spooling out along Rue 14-Février-1952. She followed him, let herself be carried away by the rhythms of the Ka, and she responded to the enchanted call of Charly the drum master. Their musical conversation went on and on, longer than the dialogue between the Ka and every previous *lewoz* dancer up to that night. Evelyn's feet were in perfect harmony with every beat Charly hit on the Ka. With every strike of the drum Evelyn struck back with a deep movement from her hips. Each step she took was matched by a sound from Charly's drum. He called, she responded. She threw down a rhythmic challenge with her body, and he responded with a blast of sounds that she immediately reproduced with more movements from her body. She let herself be possessed by the all-powerful Ka until the drum achieved total control over her. She danced like a bewitched goddess and finally collapsed in the middle of the circle that had formed around her. For a long time, she stayed that way, eyes closed, legs splayed out, torso thrown back, still in a trance as if she had surrendered completely to the Ka drum and its master. It was as if she had let herself be possessed, penetrated by the music that had taken and retaken her in staccato notes, transported her

Manor's Alley

to a paroxysm of pleasure then dropped her there, blip, like a ripe breadfruit, with no will and feeling completely weak in the knees. Everyone knew then that those two, or rather those three, would finish the night together and consummate the passion at whose birth they had all been invisible witnesses. Many of the young women who were there that night went away with shoulders slouched, hands crossed behind their back, some with a head aching from rage and jealousy, others grabbing their stomach where at that very instant they felt again the many kicks given by some tiny life that had been planted in their mother-womb and would, in the end, join the club of fatherless *sans-papas* children on this island that had never claimed its rightful soul. They had been warned many times: Charly was married to his Ka, and he pledged allegiance to it alone. That little *Anglaise* newcomer would come to understand it all too well.

So, one after the other, the core of drummers, the *tanbouyé*, went away, shaking their heads in jealousy. That Charly's still got it! Yet again, a new prize who could not resist his charm and the spell he cast! Charly found himself then with Evelyn, both of them alone in the town's plaza, two steps away from the sea that continued to sing its nocturnal complaint and caress their faces with a fresh veil of mist that delicately laid salty droplets on their thirsty lips. These droplets contained the savor of Guadeloupe and they both took pleasure drinking it in, lip-to-lip, as foreplay to an imminent body-to-body encounter. Charly took her by the hand and led her toward the beach. In the refreshing water of the Baie du Moule, he pulled her close. She gave in to him, and it was like she had fallen prey to the hypnotic charm of the Ka master. Their bodies moved in staccato rhythms and the ripples awakened little fish who witnessed things they still talk about to this day.

Evelyn still talks painfully of the events that followed that cursed day when she let herself be possessed by that island, by that music, and by that Ka master. Charly's mother, who had also witnessed this exchange, quickly demanded that she be placed with another family. The director of the exchange program who accompanied the group accused her of being a shameless young woman who had no respect for Jamaica. Furthermore, he threatened to send her home if he could not find a new host family. As for Charly, after spending the entire day sleeping (since his mother had no intention of waking him up or reprimanding him) he got up in the middle of the afternoon and sat down at the dining room table where a nice plate of fish court-bouillon and white rice seasoned with a hot *Bonda-Man-Jak* pepper was already waiting for him. He ate until he was full, said neither hello nor thank you to his mother, and headed out to the shed where he met up with his crew. At first, they received him with a slightly reproachful silence, but they quickly forgot that incident. As soon as Charly's fingers drew sound from his all-powerful Ka drum, everyone let themselves be swept away by the intoxicating music. *Répondè* and *tanbouyé* were swallowed up in the same cadences, and none of them thought anything about that young girl. Charly himself had already reached another dimension, following a musical note that carried his soul, flying and floating away. Like a musical zombie, he drifted beyond the island of Guadeloupe to a place where he encountered who knows what god of the Ka drum that would place him under his spell again and again.

Fortunately for Evelyn, Man Sonsson, an old woman from the neighborhood who needed the money, quickly volunteered to host her. It was she, moreover, who explained to Evelyn what had really happened that night and who encouraged her not to pay any attention to the remarks that all the young women made as they passed her in the streets or in stores. She had to remain strong because she was, after all, a woman who had two breasts and a strong back to carry them. "*Famn tonbé pa janmen dézèspéré,*" Man Sonsson told her: "A fallen woman never despairs." What's done was done, and it was all according to the will of the Good Lord who watches over everything. So, after their *lewoz* adventure, and even after sharing their intimacy at the beach and letting the ocean see the most intimate parts of their bodies, Charly never addressed a single word to Evelyn. He did not even defend her when his mother kicked her out of their home carrying only her little suitcase with a large Jamaican flag pasted on each side.

When she returned to Jamaica, after that three-month stay in Guadeloupe, after vomiting her guts out every morning to the point where she practically could not swallow any food (she could not even stand the smell of roast pork that her old landlady Man Sonsson had made every Saturday), Evelyn was indeed happy to find responses to the applications she had sent to the University of Florida and the University of Central Florida before departing for Guadeloupe. Her goal had been to finish her language and marketing classes there. It was with joy and relief that she read the opening lines of the first letter from UCF: *"Dear Ms. Winthrop: Congratulations! You're a Knight! . . ."* She did not even bother to open the second letter since UCF had already offered her a full scholarship that would allow her to study there with all expenses paid. On top of that, her school in Kingston was offering her a scholarship to cover housing and books! This meant that she was a remarkable student. Her curriculum vitae revealed her excellent grades but also her global knowledge not only of the Antilles but Europe and Africa as well. She had a very impressive record that showed a young woman who took an interest in her milieu but also took time to volunteer at several charities. In fact, that letter could not have come at a better time. She wanted to get away from Jamaica as soon as possible in order to avoid confessing her shame to her parents. This news of a pregnancy would kill her mother, and who knew what her father would do since he had warned her mother that it was madness to send such a young girl into the clutches of those small island negroes who were just waiting to bite into her young and tender flesh. She had to leave—fast!

As soon as she was back in Kingston, Evelyn had invented the idea that there was an internship opportunity at Walt Disney World that she could not refuse. She insisted to her parents that it was absolutely necessary to be there in person to present her candidacy because they would not consider her application unless she already lived in Orlando. So, after two weeks with her parents, she headed off quickly for the United States, leaving behind a mother in tears and a father who could not understand any of what had happened to his family. Days after her departure he was still shaking his head. He had not seen this study abroad possibility coming. He did not understand why his daughter could not stay in Jamaica to find a good man who would take care of her and a good job at the post office. Why did she have to go far away to Guadeloupe, that mosquito-filled island from which nothing good ever came, and then migrate to the United States, that huge foreign country that gluttonously devoured all Black people, ripping away their humanity with the bang of a gavel in the name of "justice"! *Bloodclat!*

Her mother, for her part, cried every day. She felt guilty about having planted the desire for independence in her daughter's soul. Very early in her daughter's life as a young woman thirsting for knowledge, she had made Evelyn understand that she controlled her own destiny and did not need to accept things as they were presented to her. She wanted to be sure that her daughter would never be enslaved in a kitchen or in one of those so-called "women's roles" that meant being mistress of the house but nothing more. She had emphasized education as the key to freedom for women and over the years she had made Evelyn understand that she was also in charge of her sexuality. She was never to be ashamed of her desires because the Good Lord Himself had placed them in her. If her bodily pleasures were sacred, she had no need to fear them. She wanted to make sure that Evelyn understood she was responsible for her own happiness and that she should not allow herself to be

Manor's Alley

trapped by men who thought only of controlling women. And now her daughter had once again moved far away from her, far away from her protection. She would not have the chance to spend more time with her, to talk about the future, about men, about children . . . She was gone . . . When would she be coming back? Fortunately, Evelyn was a strong young woman! She had certainly been brought up correctly and exposed to the truth. That was her relief. Between us, though, that means she had never thought about the power of the Ka drum, much less the *gwo* Ka!

Evelyn fled Jamaica carrying her shame hidden deep inside herself. Nevertheless, every time they hit an air pocket during the flight, she remembered that night when she had lost her reason, when she had, in spite of herself, given in wholeheartedly to a man she thought she would fall in love with, just like all the others who had lost their minds before her. She had only spent two days in his house! What spirit had seized her to make her disrespect herself in such a way? What was she going to do with this baby who would soon be born? And her studies? The next pocket the BWIA plane hit threw her forward so violently that she could not stop a jet of vomit from flying out of her mouth with force. Fortunately, the woman in the next seat handed Evelyn a brown bag and she spewed into it what felt like the very soul of a young pregnant girl whose womb was paying dues to a man she probably would never see again. What would she say to this child? She began crying so hard that her long sobs attracted the attention of all the passengers who began turning their heads toward her. "*Raaaasssss! Wat wrung wid di pikney, mon?*" Some of them concluded that this girl was in pain and that her pain was surely caused by the fact that she had left her parents for the first time. Others shook their heads and looked down on her with a judgmental air, sucking their teeth, *tsik tsik tsik* followed very quickly by a *tchiiip!* Of course, it goes without saying that her tears had given the signal to every child on the plane to start screaming and crying in unison. If this had been a film and you were in the audience you certainly would have started laughing at how comical it was to see the hostesses running from one end of the plane to the other handing out candies, lollipops, bottles of water, milk, everything they could put their hands on to pacify the situation. Evelyn heard "*Quiet*" coming from every corner of the plane. "*Shut yuh mout, ooman!*"

Camille and Jean-Luc, who were coming back from a series of conferences organized by the World Up Now company at the Hyatt Ziva Rose hotel in Kingston, could not believe their eyes. As Camille refused to travel in a private jet, Jean-Luc had tried without success to obtain a place in first class that would allow them to have more space to stretch their legs. Moreover, the young man who had given them their boarding pass had replied with a smirk, "Everybody flies first class with British West Indies Airlines!" So they found themselves seated next to this young woman who hadn't stopped crying since the plane departed. Camille suspected with certainty that she was sick with grief. She could have asked to change places, but the plane was full to bursting and she suspected that no one would want to take her seat. Jean-Luc had put on his headphones and was nodding his head, probably to the rhythm of his hero, the late Patrick Saint-Eloi, or Bob Marley. Nothing ever upset him. He never seemed to let events get the better of him. Camille observed the girl. She looked lonely, abandoned, and homesick. Something stirred in her heart and she felt she had to get closer and make a connection. She touched the girl lightly with her finger and she let out a big sigh that seemed to calm her down. She took a few deep breaths and started to shake. The girl now had goosebumps and was sweating big drops of sweat despite the air conditioning. The plane was now quiet, and a stewardess approached the row where Camille and her neighbor were seated. With a look, without saying a word, she confirmed with

Camille that from here on everything would be fine. Camille handed her the brown airsickness bag with her fingertips and replied with a simple gesture of her clenched fist with her thumb pointing upward, letting the hostess know that things were going better.

The young woman laid her head instinctively on Camille's chest, who immediately covered her with the shawl that she wore around her neck.

"What's your name?" Camille asked her.

"Eh-vu-lynh," she replied between sobs.

Camille then took the girl in her arms and began to caress her forehead, her temples, then the straightened hair that was now clinging to her forehead. Evelyn fell asleep in the arms of Camille, who had to wake her up when they arrived at the Sanford airport. Jean-Luc had made fun of Camille during the rest of the trip, telling her that she was acting like a mother-hen and that she had to detach herself from this young girl before becoming attached to her forever.

"Wake up Evelyn! Wake up!"

The young girl woke up with a start, surprised to find herself in the arms of a stranger. A dark spot on Evelyn's collar showed where she had been drooling while she slept.

"Oh Laaawwwd have mercy! I'm so sorry ma'am, I'm so sorry!"

"Don't worry about it," Camille replied in a strong French accent. "Is your family coming to pick you up?" Evelyn began crying again, this time silently.

"No ma'am! I've got nobody and I have no idea where I'm going. I'll see if I can get a cab to get me to some hotel so I can figure out my life. Thank you so much for your help." She replied without lifting her head a single time, without ever looking Camille or Jean-Luc in the eye.

Without even asking him anything, Camille turned to Jean-Luc, who nodded and swept the air with a wave of his right hand that meant: "I have nothing to say about that anyway." He knew her heart. He knew that she had immediately decided to take charge of this girl so that no other person would come and take advantage of her innocence. She had met so many young women caught in the clutches of these pimps who knew how to find women that life had left by the wayside if only for a few moments. The Don't Touch My Girl Center she created ten years ago had seen its share of lost young souls come and collapse at its doors like birds with broken wings. She refused no one and did everything for her daughters, as she called them. Many of them, once rehabilitated and well established, refused to leave and served as mentors to new arrivals.

"I tell you what," said Camille. "Why don't you come with us today so you can figure out a plan. I don't feel good leaving you here at the airport on your own. Is it your first time in the state?"

"Oui, Madame," Evelyn responded timidly.

"Oh you speak French?"

"Yes, I speak it quite fluently," she continued in French. "I speak Kreyol too."

"But you are Jamaican, no?"

"Yes, of course! But I studied French in school and I visited Guadeloupe many times and even lived there for three months."

Immediately after saying these last words, Evelyn nearly fainted from weakness. She could no longer stand on her legs. Jean-Luc caught her at the right moment, just before she collapsed on the ground. He looked at Camille, who seemed ready to cry too. He directed them to the outside of the airport where their driver, Ramon, already waiting for them, hastened to take care of their luggage.

"What is your full name, young lady?" Jean-Luc asked Evelyn.

"Winthrop. Evelyn Winthrop. Thank you very much," she responded, still completely enveloped in her cloud.

"Ramon, grab her luggage as well. How many pieces of luggage, mademoiselle?"

"Two," she replied. "Two large ones. They're red."

Manor's Alley

Jean-Luc shook his head and rolled his eyes upward. "Aaah! Women! Always too much luggage! What's she carrying around in two big suitcases? She's so small!"

Ramon came back quickly accompanied by another young man who was dragging a large cart on which he had put all the suitcases. Camille alone had four of them! They arrived at the right time as a security guard was walking toward them, blowing shrill blasts on his whistle and telling them that they were forbidden to park in front of the exit terminal. Luckily for them, everyone was already settled in and ready to go. Ramon discretely placed a twenty dollar bill in the hands of the young porter and whispered in his ear, *"Pa'l niño, hermano.* For your child," and got behind the wheel.

"Thanks, man! *Que Dios te bendiga!"* the young man said while quickly sliding the bill into his pocket.

The forty-five minute ride to the Chamberlain residence was done in great silence. Jean-Luc continued to listen to his music, answered a few phone calls, and returned to his music while tapping on his iPad with two sticks that he always had with him.

"Your trip to Quebec is confirmed. We have to be there on the seventeenth of next month. I think we'll have to rent an apartment in Paris for a few days because we won't have time to go home then leave two days later for Canada."

"Okay Jean-Luc," answered Camille. "You tell me where I should be and when I should be there and I'm there. It's quite simple. There are no problems. Are there any candidates coming to see about the position today?"

"No, not today. Besides, I've had enough. No one meets the criteria you have imposed so far. None of the candidates I interviewed speak the three languages fluently, and even if they do speak at least one, they do not know how to write it. I'm willing to give them a pass for Kreyol, I myself do not know how to write it. But at least French! It shouldn't be that hard to find someone who can speak English,

25

French, and Kreyol with knowledge of business and marketing . . ."

At these words, they both turned at the same time toward Evelyn who was resting in the backseat of the black Lincoln.

She looked at them both with her gleaming, black almond eyes, coated in tears that would not flow and instead formed like a cushion of air around the whites of her eyes. She replied simply by throwing back her head, which bounced on the soft headrest, her arms relaxed, as if broken by the pain inside her:

"*An ansent . . . Twa mwa*—I'm three months pregnant!"

Jean-Luc and Camille both looked at her open-mouthed for a moment that seemed like an eternity.

Jean-Luc was the first to break the silence and asked: "And your parents . . ." He was not able to finish his sentence because Camille had just elbowed him in the stomach, forcing him to lose his breath and nearly choke. He turned around in his seat, holding his stomach while aiming an inquisitive look at Camille, who was now holding Evelyn's hand in her own. He would definitely never understand anything about women. How could he guess that it was not polite to ask such a logical question to this young lady they had just met. She had almost vomited her whole body on his wife two hours ago and now Camille was already treating her as if she were her daughter! Man, oh man! he thought, shaking his head.

"Don't worry, my child," said Camille. "It's not by chance that the universe placed you next to us on the flight. We are going to find a solution, together." She gave Jean-Luc a firm look, and he could only smile in response. He knew his wife. He was going to trust her. So many times he had doubted her. He had always had to pay her back with something, some jewelry, some new wardrobe, some trip. This time, he would be careful not to contradict her! It was starting to cost him too much, and at this thought he smiled again.

They soon arrived at their villa. The portal opened automatically and revealed Manor's Alley. Evelyn closed and opened her eyes several times, turned her head toward Camille and asked under her breath: "Who are you?"

"*Moun Lakou*," Camille replied simply. "Yard people from Monbruno Court!"

Evelyn clenched her fists. She wanted to pinch herself but she didn't dare, for fear of appearing stupid in the eyes of these two people who had come to her aid in such a . . . miraculous way.

Aware of her great astonishment, Camille hastened to add: "We haven't always lived at this level or in this kind of milieu. I'll tell you all about it . . .," murmured Camille, her gaze fixed far ahead of her, as if her thoughts had reached another border, another time, a time of yard people, the *moun lakou* . . .

part two

Monbruno Court

"FOR AS LONG AS I CAN REMEMBER, I always disliked Monbruno Court," Camille began. "I never felt like I was a part of that world. Yet wasn't I among the poorest and most deprived of this place? Was I not a product of it? Mother had me there. I was that stolen pleasure robbed from her innocent youth. And I stayed inside of her, clutching to the sides of her entrails, sole witness to her pain, the only result of that unhappy rainy day when her only mistake had been to ask for "a little shelter from the rain, please, *Mésié-dam bonjou*! Good evening Sir, Mam!"

She went on like that every day for at least two hours, continuing her story, planted in her favorite chair facing the orchard of tropical fruit trees (more than a hundred varieties) that Jean-Luc had planted along the lake that formed the border of their Chamberlain Estate property. She told her story and Evelyn transcribed it, page after page . . .

A Spider's Web

Une toile d'araignée

NARROW AND FILLED WITH POTHOLES, my street seemed to me like a serpent that stretched lazily from one end of the neighborhood to the other. It had the feel of a sassy woman, swaying her hips from side to side as if chanting, "this side for you, that side for me," searching for the next prey, one who would fall victim to its numbing venom. Monbruno Court was neither straight nor crooked, it just had that look. From its hips, other smaller arteries stretched out and disappeared in all directions. It was a veritable spider's web where many lives were lost, swallowed up in the hungry guts of poverty.

The neighborhood street was flanked by little houses, all of them topped with corrugated tin roofs shaped like an inverted V. The men and women inside were like headless crabs whose eyes could only gaze backward into their own life of poverty, and that roofing was all that separated them from the biting sun of Guadeloupe. There they all simmered in a dirty river of their own sweat, reproducing with no hope of a better tomorrow. "Tomorrow, God willing," they all said, and tomorrow always arrived but without ever pleasing

God. And so it was. And the children saw, and they heard, and they understood, and they accepted. And that was the meaning of life! All of it like a toothless mouth opening up to reveal a few decayed stumps, that is how the lakou appeared to me with all its houses in teeming poverty.

The street seemed more welcoming when you looked at it from the main road. It seemed to invite you in. Its mouth opened wide the better to swallow those who were unfortunate enough to linger there, narrowing little by little, multiplying itself in the numerous little side streets where the path got so small that even the Citroen 2CVs could not get through. In this way, the lakou stifled its inhabitants, who remained its prisoners, so to speak. It was like a snake that swallows it prey little by little, bathing them in a paralyzing venom of poverty that sticks to your skin.

The dusty little shop of Man Lestie was the first one in the street. It was jammed in between the house of her sister Lorna, whose enormous feet were swollen by elephantiasis, and the house with a porch that belonged to Madame Célutin. Across from that was the house of Téléna who had lost her youngest daughter in some truly bizarre way, dead but no one knew how or from what malady. Téléna was never the same after the death of her baby and had more or less gone insane. She buried herself in silence and never spoke another word to anyone, not even to my mother who had been her closest friend. Thérèse's house was both bizarre and interesting. In fact, she rented it from Monsieur Célutin who lived just across the street. Everyone knew there was history between them, stories of money, of unpaid debts, and threats to put it all out in the street. To enter her house, you had to step over a little creek or rather, a little canal that carried in it all the waters used by the entire neighborhood. As a little girl, this canal seemed deep and wide to me. Thinking of it now, I realize it was not much bigger than two adult footsteps. After crossing over the little bridge in front of her entrance, we stepped

A Spider's Web

down into a small interior porch that was actually an unfinished room with a missing wall. The cement floor was always cool, which meant I always found it a good place to play whenever my mother would visit there. To get into the main house, you had to climb two steps to another entrance that opened into a very simple interior behind a curtain of multicolored hanging blinds. I never had the chance to look beyond the main table in that room. Everything I could perceive there had the look of impenetrable mysteries, of shapes and scents that inspired my childish imagination.

Further down in the neighborhood, after crossing a tiny sailor's bridge that could barely be distinguished from the rest of the block, and beneath which flowed the miserable waters of the neighborhood people, one came to the store of Monsieur and Madame Coquin. They were a couple who had set up there, in Monbruno Court, and who ran their little store and rumshop. Apparently, one of their daughters was my godmother but I never saw her and she never made any effort to fulfil her godmotherly duties (which consisted, from what I gathered, in looking after me if my mother was not able). How many times I thought she could have offered me at least a cute white panty to cover my entire backside! So many times, I had to make due with some aunt's sexy panties because I had grown bigger and my own were torn to pieces.

The shop-house of Monsieur and Madame Coquin served as a hub in Monbruno Court. At their place, we learned everything that had happened from the beginning of the street where it connected to National Route 20 to where it met the road that led to Madame Felix's boutique. Back then, the Coquin's house was divided into four rooms. The front part that opened onto the road contained the little store where my mother sent me to do the shopping. The room in the back served as the rumshop, and their bedroom was, I think, the room next to the rumshop. In the interior courtyard, separated from the house by a small service hallway, and to the side of the rumshop, there was a stuffy and humid room that served as a warehouse and where they piled up all sorts of empty boxes, cases, bottles, cartons, and whats-not. In the rear courtyard, they raised rabbits in a large hutch, and chickens that shat out fresh eggs every morning. In a room detached from the rest of the house, they had their kitchen with an icebox. A large rectangle of wood, humid and blackened with mold, the icebox held in its breast and buried in immense blocks of translucent ice five-franc and two-franc treasures that were frozen, mummified in their coat of ice, leaving only their silhouette to appear, craved by buyers of all ages. To dislodge these treasures, they used an icepick. The pick was a sharply pointed iron bar, that could, in the fist of Monsieur or Madame Coquin, shatter into thousands of pieces that ice that had the power to lengthen the life of food and unleash the flavor of drinks, Fanta orange, Royal red, and Ordinaire lemonade.

Aaaaah! Ordinaire lemonade. That was my favorite. Well chilled, it offered pure ecstasy! That licorice flavor would go straight down your throat and quench your thirst fast, 3-2-1! There was nothing ordinary about Ordinaire lemonade . . . And yet, I have to admit that it was the kind of thing that only made sense in the time capsule of my childhood. In later years, after having lived outside the country, far from the lakou, I rediscovered my Ordinaire lemonade. Unfortunately, it had changed, or rather, I had changed, and I never knew how to recover the sweet and spicy flavor that had previously left me speechless. It had become for me a simple ordinary lemonade whose taste irritated the tongue and whose sugar poisoned the spirit. And I found myself surprised to be so attached to a drink that was so . . . ordinary.

Vegetable Soup

Soupe aux légumes

A LITER OF KEROSENE, a quarter-pound of smoked bacon, a quarter-pound of salted cod, a little can of tomato sauce, and a half-pound of rice. I loved the taste of pork that had been dried and smoked and could never resist it. So much so that, often enough, I would reach home with the four sides of a piece of bacon nibbled away, bitten as if a rat had attacked it. I knew that I was going to get thrashed but the smell of smoked bacon was too strong to resist. Monsieur Coquin always made sure to offer me a little bit of smoked bacon just for myself, really to help me avoid those beatings. Madame Coquin was always too stingy to give me anything.

It was the same thing with Viandox, those cubes of beef bouillon we used for Sunday night soup. I would carefully open the goldfoil packaging and bite off just a small edge from one of the corners. There were enough corners on the cube that mother was certainly not going to notice it. The problem was that I was never satisfied with only one corner, and many times I would get back to the house with only half a cube. Needless to say, on those days, the soup was ruined and my backside was more peeled than the carrots, the potatoes, the leeks, and the cabbage that she had taken so

37

much pain to cut in very tiny, regular pieces. Her fingers are still very lacerated, even to this day.

I have to say that soup in our house was an important part of the weekly routine. Mother sat herself at the wooden table in the kitchen and peeled and chopped up the carrots, leeks, potatoes, squash, celery, and turnips into diced, cubed, sliced, or ring-shaped cuts. I was always fascinated by her way of cutting all the vegetables to a certain thickness according to their variety. Most of all, I loved the way she diced the orange carrots. Patiently, she cut them all in the same size, the same precision. Once all the vegetables were cut, she threw them in her big black stewpot whose bottom was as big as our neighbor Celestine's butt. The pot was boiling so strongly it made sounds like *gwo Ka* and *cadence rampa* music. Mom had added a pig foot and beef bones she had bought from Madame Liparo, the neighborhood butcher who lived just across from us.

In this way, the soup simmered ever so slowly on the charcoal stove that sat like a king in the little corner we used as our kitchen. Our first stove was nothing more than a big paint can that a neighbor had happened to convert into an oven. The inside of the pot had been coated to a good thickness with cement, and there was a hole in the middle in which we placed pieces of charcoal. Near the bottom, the can had been pierced with an opening big enough to serve as an air vent to let out the smoke. I really think the Europeans were inspired by our model when they built their modern electric ovens . . . or maybe it was the other way around! Little by little, we added just enough charcoal to cook the meal to perfection. In my memories, the best congo soups, the best *bébélé* dumpling stews, the most sumptuous breadfruit and crab soups were simmered to perfection on the charcoal cookstoves of my childhood.

The marriage of those different colors and flavors resulted in a smooth, creamy soup that I liked to savor on a Sunday night while it was still warm. And woe unto me if I let it cool off or if mother

Vegetable Soup

was late in serving it to me. Then a thick layer of fat and grease would form on the surface of my soup and congeal on my lips. I still remember one night when she gave me cold soup. I heard them, my mother and stepfather, laughing and frolicking behind the house. She scrubbed his back while splashing water on him. They had nerve to be enjoying themselves even though I was dying of hunger. What was it she saw in him, anyway? What was he doing to her that she would give in to such childishness? She who never took me in her arms and never looked me in the eyes? What miracle transformed her into a young woman whose voice I could not even recognize? You would think that she had finally found happiness! Maybe this was what men did for women? Explosions of laughter sparkled like fireworks then vanished in the black sky of Monbruno Court.

Sitting there, by myself, I tried to forget about my hunger by hunting the mosquitos that were feasting on my blood, sip by tiny sip. I was hungry with a hunger that gnawed at my insides. I don't know how long I waited that night for my mother to come and feed me, but it seemed like an eternity. I could not understand how my mother could deliberately choose to have a good time with a man rather than coming to take care of her only child who was dying of hunger. I was whining so much—"*Maman*, I'm hungry"—that she finally and unwillingly came in to feed me.

I heard the sound of heavy and agitated footsteps approaching. They rattled the knotholes in the wood floor of our two-room shack. I knew from the lumbering rhythm of her step that she was not happy. Her inaudible words made a grumbling noise in our corner kitchen. Then she appeared in the shadowy light of the kerosene lamp and placed before me a bowl of soup. The surface looked like an ice-skating rink like the ones I had seen in my French reading books. I stared at the soup. It was cold. The grease from the beef bone she had used to season the soup had hardened in places into a thick, crackled layer. The diced cubes of carrots and squash were now petrified in that skating rink ice and I could not even distinguish slices of celery from diced potatoes. I lifted my head and looked at my mother in the light of our kerosene lamp and I heard myself say . . . in fact, the words flew out of my mouth . . . oh! unhappy day that I will regret for the rest of my life:

"*Lè ou tini soup fligé aw pou ban mwen*—Don't ever serve me cold soup again—you took time to make it, but you couldn't give me some—*sé pa la pèn ban mwen'y?*"

Before I had even finished the sentence, I was struck with a volley of blows all over my back, as if the goddess Kali had thrown herself upon me with all her many arms. And I heard my mother's voice say: "*An ké apran vou rèspèkté mwen isidan*—You *will* learn to respect me in this house." "*Sa an ba'w, sé sa ou ka manjé*—What I serve you is what you will eat." "*Ki mafouti kouyonad é sa*—What rude-ass wickedness is this?" and "*Ki kalité lang ou ka palé ban mwen la, an ké fè'y rantré an goj aw*—What kind of language is that for you to be speaking to me? I'll make you swallow those words!"

Each word came with a blow on my head, on my back, on my little girl's body. After what seemed like an interminable time, my stepfather came to save me from the truncheon hands of my mother. I don't need to add that I never again tried out such lines on her. In hindsight, I understood that I had certainly interrupted one of my mother's few moments of happiness. Come to think of it, she was only twenty-eight years old then, and had not known many moments of joy. I never again heard those eruptions of open laughter coming from my mother's throat. Some years later, that stepfather who had shielded me from my Kali-goddess-mother was gone from our life. He left for France like so many other Black men before him, chasing the dream of a better life, far from the asphalt roofs that up to then had kept him stuck in the shipyards of Canacini, where he labored under the merciless sun of Guadeloupe. And I wondered . . .

Besides the soup, other times it was just a quarter-pound of

Vegetable Soup

salted cod and a half-pound of rice to make *diri wouj* or red rice that my mother would send me to buy at Monsieur Coquin's place. When we had a meal of *diri wouj*, I knew that days of deprivation were coming soon. That meant we would not have any extra money to go and buy blood sausage at the Liparos' on Saturday evening. With all the heat given off by our tin roof, and no refrigerator, that would also mean that we had to put up with eating the rest of the *diri wouj* which would have certainly spoiled by the end of the day. Just as I learned to comb the water in our barrel to get rid of frog eggs and mosquito larvae that had settled there, in the same way my mother taught me to sort through the food in order to avoid the slimy pieces that signaled the rice was no longer good to eat.

It was a very simple but delicate process. With the aid of a fork or spoon, I learned to pick up a small bit of rice to inspect its freshness. When I lifted the spoon, if a viscous string was hanging from it like a spider's web, it meant that piece of rice had gone off. It did not mean, however, that we had to throw out the rest of the food. No, no, no! There was always a portion of the rice that remained edible. One could not throw away food just like that, not food the Good Lord had given us! Come on now! And if, by accident, I consumed one or two mouthfuls of sticky rice, I surely was not going to die from it. I'm still here, aren't I?

Diri wouj on the menu also meant that we did not have money to buy any beef on Sunday at the butcher. Without meat, there would be no red beans and rice for the Sunday meal and above all no pan-roasted meat on the stove. Weekends were looking pretty rough.

That *diri wouj* was one of the simplest meals to prepare in our house. All we needed was some rice and tomato sauce. Of course, we had to add some spices like chives, parsley, thyme, onion, and garlic with a little bit of vinegar. If we did not have any hot pepper or were missing some spices, all we had to do was knock on the door of Eloise or Amie Marceline, one of my mother's very few trusted *commères*, and we would get what we needed, no problem. These two women were the only ones my mother had as close friends. She would always say: "*Mwen, an pakay aka pon moun*—Me, I'm not going inside anyone's house." "*Dayè, sé toujou chez toi, jamais chez moi*—Of course, it's always your house, never mine!" "*Zanmi sé malédisyon. Sé zafè a bab*—Friends are a curse, they're trouble!" And that is a lesson I still keep buried deep inside myself to this day.

We browned the spices in a good slug of Alba oil. Into this mix, which we spiced up even more with a nice hot *Bonda-Man-Jak* pepper, we would add a little tomato sauce and if we wanted it, some crumbled up salt cod. Once the tomato sauce was blended with the cod and spices, we added about three cups of water and brought it all to a boil. Finally, we added the rice, and voilà! I learned then to appreciate that the *diri wouj* established the rhythmic flow of my life and conveyed messages about our condition as yard people— *moun lakou*—that my mother never needed to explain to me. It was, by the way, the first meal I learned how to prepare on our three-legged kerosene stove. Yes, progress had smiled on my mother and me! From working as a maid and housekeeper for some Whites in town, she had earned a small income and finally was able to buy a kerosene stove! I still ask myself how I was able to avoid a fiery accident. Once when the stove's container was full of kerosene, we added a little alcohol to burn in the reservoir at the top. We had to pump the kerosene to get the fire started and we did that by striking a match at the level of the reservoir with the alcohol in it. Then, the blonde flame escaped through the head of the stove with a *whump* that sounded like an angry neighborhood woman. It spread out through all the holes on the burner, giving off a bluish flame wrapped in yellow-gold lace that reminded me of sunsets. Sometimes, I had to pump the stove to rekindle the flame, all the while making sure the "canary" stove remained balanced on its three legs. Little by little the stove became the symbol and sign

Vegetable Soup

of our progress as lakou women, but in my heart I still longed for the smoky savor of meals cooked on our charcoal stove. I have to admit that our life in Monbruno Court was often time-stamped by the cries of children who had been burned accidentally when a kerosene stove tipped over. Because of this, my relationship with that machine was a rapport ruled by respect and fear. I knew that the more I pumped it full of air, the more it could end up spitting fire into my face one day.

Before getting to the Coquin's shop, you first had to pass by the house of Monsieur Couchi! He was my favorite. Thanks to the music he played at full volume, because he was the only one who had a turntable, I always knew exactly which season it was. I loved when it was Christmas and he began to play the seasonal songs. The sound of that record player laid down the beat of our lives in the lakou. Every night, and especially on Saturdays, he would play "Amour, bonheur, et louange" or "Allez mon voisin." After Christmas, it would be Carnival season with its devilish masks covered in tar and spiky quills. Next, Easter and stations of the cross, or processions of Black people beating their chests on Vergain Hill, repeating over and over, "Through my fault, through my fault, through my most grievous fault," while following a miserable cross dragged by an equally miserable volunteer who represented Our Savior Jesus Christ. Then finally the period of long vacations would come. This would be announced by the arrival of many Guadeloupeans who came back to us rolling their Rs, some with children whose skin was much more powdery and light than our own shades of ebony black and sapotille brown. We were expected to keep a certain distance from them in order to show them the respect that was apparently their right upon returning! After all, they were returning from France, the mother country that knew how to transform Blacks into educated and evolved men or women who could no longer tell a crab from a conger eel, and who also had lost the taste for congo

43

soup and the breadfruit that thickened it! They came back to us completely dressed up in the French of *Fwans*, and this gave them the right to think of us as backward primitives with no future as we were (to them) more or less imprisoned behind the bars of our Kreyol. They fascinated me! And again, I wondered . . .

Monsieur and Madame Couchi's house was another enigma. No one ever went in or out. All day long, both of them sat in front of the unique little entryway that framed their universe. There they laid out on a little stool a basket stocked with mangos, breadfruit, yams, guineps, and so on, that they happily sold to those who had not been able to get to the market that day. I never knew where they got those items, but by the end of the day they had always sold everything. I tend to think they lived off of the sale of produce they grew themselves because I never saw them coming or going to any store in the area.

Directly across from the Couchis was the great house of Monsieur Monbruno. I think it was because he had the biggest house in the area that the neighborhood bore his name. He lived there with his wife, a grande dame with beige skin the color of a ripe sapotille, or maybe a bit darker, who always wore her wavy hair in four large plaits. It was a hairstyle that made her head seem a little square shaped. She was also a bit large, but her size was distributed throughout her grande dame body that she always covered up by wearing a large creole dress that actually added to the squarish shape created by the large plaits on her head. The Monbrunos' house was, so to speak, the festival hall of the neighborhood. The iron grill door at the front of their residence opened into a large room that had tables and chairs like a restaurant. At the back of the room, Madame Monbruno had a small shop where she sold a little of everything, especially alcohol. However, my mother never sent me to the Monbrunos to buy any of the things we needed. Instead, she sent me to the Coquins or Madame Félix even though her store

Vegetable Soup

was located farther down the street. When I thought about it, my best guess was that she did this for several reasons. The first was that the Coquins were our neighbors and their daughter was my godmother. So that was like saying we were part of the same family! They had witnessed all of my mother's suffering and they knew she was an honest woman. The second reason was that Madame Félix also knew very well what our situation was and never had a problem extending little credits that mother promised to repay as quickly as possible. Mother never waited for the little ledger book with square lines in which Madame Félix carefully marked down all the commission that we bought at her place to get too full. She hated to buy things on credit and made me understand it well. The third and perhaps the real reason was the type of crowd that frequented the Monbrunos' place. I never saw anyone there but men who had spent their entire day drinking and drinking some more. On the weekend, the restaurant-rumshop changed into a dance hall where the neighborhood people met to dance to the latest records by Paul Blamar, Moune de Rivel, and Emilien Otile.

Monsieur Monbruno himself was a man with dark skin and a smooth bald head. He wore white shorts like the overseer of a plantation domain and had the air of someone important who knew how to give orders with the tips of his fingers. Over the years, I came to understand from conversations of all the *nèg a ronm*, the rum-soaked drunkards from the shop, that he was the son of someone who owned the land that we all lived on. He probably lived off the rent money he received from some of us. Mother and I, we did not pay anything, or maybe someone had paid at the beginning when the family had put down the house on this little patch of land that we occupied up to now. It was not uncommon at the time to see a house transported by large truck from one place to another. In the Guadeloupe of that epoch, we did not simply carry our furniture when we moved. The entire house with all its contents would be uprooted and deposited on some other ground, resting on four big rocks. It was quite simple.

Monsieur Monbruno always enjoyed the status of a master in the lakou. He had the respect of all the neighborhood residents. I never knew if he had children or family. He and his wife remained for me strange characters who operated on another wavelength, one where things were very different from our daily lives as lakou people. We never bought anything at all there. And that's how it was!

The Bator family lived next door to the Monbrunos. This family was very unusual. None of them would join in the daily life of Monbruno Court. There were quite a few of them, girls and boys, each one not much bigger than the others, like stair steps. People said they were Jehovah's Witnesses. This simple label placed them in a category of untouchables. Nobody would mix with their life and neither would they have anything to do with anybody else, except in the mornings when they insisted on waking everyone up. They would go door-to-door distributing their little pamphlet that commanded us to wake up. *Awake!* was literally the title of the pamphlet that offered a picture in which you could see lions, giraffes, and all the other jungle animals living in harmony with people of the earth. Moreover, the cover of the pamphlet always pictured a nice family in the middle of a savannah, surrounded by wild animals. The two children both had blonde hair, a little girl in a ponytail and her little brother whose face was sprinkled with freckles, playing with these jungle beasts under the peaceful gaze of their parents. The Bators explained that it would be healthy for us infidels to join their religion in order to maybe—if we worked hard and preached their good news—have a chance to be among the 144,000 who would be chosen to enter into the Kingdom of Jehovah! I was not familiar with any of the animals in those images. There were no racoons, no black-skinned creole pigs, and no island goats! What's more, none

Vegetable Soup

of the human characters resembled anyone that I might recognize from Monbruno Court. And again I wondered . . .

Passing the Bators' house on the right-hand side of the street—because you never looked at the houses situated on the left-hand side, or ventured to walk on the sidewalk by Man Lestie, for fear of catching elephantiasis from Lorna or having your foot twisted up like a horseshoe—you reached then to the Baduel family's house. They were a normal family with a father, a mother, girls and boys, and a grandmother who had her own house right next to the family abode. They enjoyed more luxuries than the rest of us in Monbruno Court. The Baduels had a car, electricity, running water, leather armchairs, I mean that was luxury! At school, I became friends with Joséphat, the next to last of Madame Baduel's five daughters. We frequented the same places and very often walked together along the path that led to the normal school, our elementary school.

Saturday Is Coming
for Every Little
Pig in the Country

Tout ti kochon dan bwa,
yo tout tini sanmdi a yo

"SATURDAY IS COMING FOR EVERY LITTLE PIG in the country." This saying was really true in Monbruno Court. My Saturday mornings were pierced by the harsh cries of pigs that were being killed and butchered at the Liparos', the butchers who lived across the street. As painful as it was for me to listen to the shouts from the little pigs, I always waited impatiently for Saturday afternoon so I could go buy my twenty-five centimes of spicy blood sausage at the Liparos' shop. Mother of *God that was good! Finger-licking good!*

The butcher was located across from Madame Coquin's. It was a small shack with a shutterless window. The opening served as a counter for the numerous customers who came from all over the neighboring lakous to buy their spicy blood sausage and fresh meats for Sunday lunch. Madame Liparo, in other words, really knew how to set this up right. I watched her routine many times and was disgusted, amazed, and perplexed but always delighted at the thought of the final result. Into a piece of pig intestine, she poured

Saturday Is Coming for Every Little Pig

a thick mélange of pig blood, stale breadcrumbs, chives, *Bonda-Man-Jak* pepper, four-spice, and other secret spices in a recipe that she guarded jealously. In a large zinc bucket, she stirred all of that up with the help of a *lélé*, which was a big stick made from well-polished wood that we always called "the blood sausage *lélé*!" When the mixture had taken on a dark, reddish-brown tint, and when we could no longer distinguish the chives from the pepper and the bread, then Madame Liparo armed herself with a giant funnel. She stuck this into the end of a long piece of sausage casing and with a large ladle she then began to stuff the entire length of the pig intestine with her mixture. Once this operation was finished she moved onto the next phase. For that, she needed the help of one of the children or M. Liparo.

"Franciiiiiiiiine!"

"Yes, mamaaaaannn!"

"Come, child! I need you!"

And Francine would come running, standing tip-toed on her little seven-year-old girl's feet so she could hold the sausage until her mother tied it off in smaller portions, measured by eye but measured correctly. Experience had made her a master! In later years, the Liparos got a new system that let Madame Liparo hang the larger pieces of blood sausage without anyone's help. Aaaaah, progress!

Still, this delicate operation did not stop there. All the while she was making her preparations, Madame Liparo had been tending to a charcoal fire. On it was a large stewpot with water and sprigs of chive that had just about reached the boiling point. It was, as they say, like a well-synchronized ballet. Just to the side, she had also placed a big tub of cold water. Then she turned around and took her hunk of blood sausage, poked it with a sewing needle in various places to let the grease drain out and keep the sausage from exploding. Very carefully, she dipped her prize first in the stewpot of hot water, just for a few seconds, and then in the basin of cold water. All that preparation seemed to last for an eternity, but when she finished, she hung each piece over a crockery bowl and Francine and I had the rights to all the blood sausage droppings that collected in the bowl. Our little fingers became knives and forks that we sent quickly back and forth to our mouths, each with the aim of gobbling up this bloody, spicy feast faster than the other. Man oh man, that was more finger-licking goodness, so much so I don't know how we kept from biting off our own fingers! As I could never get enough, I had to rely on my mother, depending on how well things had gone for her during the week, to go back later and buy me my own blood sausage, accompanied by some *sauce chien*, a Guadeloupean Kreyol sauce, or a nicely garnished green-bean salad. Aaaahhh! Saturdays in Monbruno Court!

Twist My Head,
Make Me Cry!

Touné tèt'ay, i ka pléré!

Fountain, no more shall I drink your water.

—MEDIEVAL PROVERB

IN MONBRUNO COURT, there were all kinds of people. Some were more poor, some were less poor, but all were poor. Those who were able to buy a Frigidaire, or to have running water, or to enjoy a TV, or even to have a car, they were among the most fortunate in the lakou. And they acted "chichi," which is another way of saying their manners were pretentious! In fact, many families were of some means. When they saw you passing with a bucket in hand on the way to fetch water, they would gaze down on you from up on high. As you passed by, they would look you up and down while muttering something inaudible or whispering secrets to each other. My mother never let it get to her. She just continued on her way, head held high, looking sharp, with her little girl following behind, leading me firmly by the hand until we reached the fountain at Fleret' Court.

Between the two lakous, we had to cross a canal full of fetid water coming from who knows where and flowing on to some equally unknown destination. The residents of Monbruno Court and those of Fleret Court whose houses had a canal view tossed all of their waste into the canal, including their urine and excrement. When it rained, we saw all sorts of debris floating there, furniture, electric appliances, rusted sheet metal, metal scraps, plastic, and so on. And when the torrential rains of the rainy season came, pouring down on our poverty as residents of the lakou, those waters became pregnant with the awful smells of our world as well as all kinds of detritus thrown into the canal from other more well off places. The waters rose up, swelled out, and exploded so much so that they seeped in during the night, always at night, into our shacks, into all the dwellings. For hours and days at a time, they became private floating islands at the mercy of the wind that alone held the possibility of carrying us to another, better place.

I was conscious of all these things and I lived them and observed them. I did not understand the reason why things were this way, but I knew in my heart that they could be different. Even so, I really enjoyed those little hikes to Fleret Court. I just had to hold my nose from time to time. Maman took her zinc bucket in one hand and my hand in the other, which she never let go of for any reason. It was as if she was afraid someone would snatch me out of her hands and take me away to who knows where. My only real worry, though, on these voyages to get water, was Crazy Renée.

She lived in the first house to the right on Fleret Court when you were coming from Monbruno. And the fountain was several meters further down under a big mango tree. Back then, passing her house was for me a delicate and dangerous test. Almost every day, Crazy Renée, a thin, light-skinned woman with good hair (as we said in the lakou) and long legs, was always standing under a breadfruit tree in front of her house. She was in the habit of littering the street with all kinds of things. If it were not buckets of

Twist My Head, Make Me Cry!

rice and beans she had spread out on the road, it was all kinds of pieces of clothing, dirty underwear, rags, filthy water she dumped there, seasoned with her dirty rants and invectives. She argued all by herself under the breadfruit tree, lashing out against all those who stopped to watch her, or she planted herself in the middle of the street gesturing with arms that were so long they reminded me of the windmills that appeared in school reading books. She was also in the habit of throwing urine on curious passersby after collecting it and letting it marinate for days in a piss-stinking white clay pot. Maman knew how to handle it. She never looked at her and shielded me with her body until we had passed Renée and her madness. After one of these encounters, I would think about Renée quite a bit, and I wondered what could have happened to make her turn out that way. One time I ask mother why Renée was crazy and she replied that once, in her youth, Renée was a beautiful, light-skinned *chabine* with good *bel chivé* hair like strands of chive who worked for the Social Security office. She had plenty of suitors but she set her sights on a married man. Having gotten wind of their affair, the wife made pilgrimage after pilgrimage, and conducted many rituals, and in a short time Renée lost her mind and her pretty *chabine* hair and never recovered them. Ultimately, she became the wreck we saw in Fleret' Court where she did daily penance for her adulterous soul. This explanation made me swear to myself that I would never steal anyone's husband. And all things considered, I felt very content with the peppercorn Black girl's hair that God had given me, even if my school friends mocked my nappy head of hair that never grew past my ears. If good hair made you wind up crazy in Fleret' Court, I would rather keep my peppercorns!

In this same street lived another unique character: Doudoute! Doudoute lived just across from the fountain where we drew our water. She was a tiny old woman with a curved back, almost a hunch-back, and lively little eyes that pierced your heart and mind, and people said she possessed magic powers. Her house was filled with impenetrable mysteries and strange odors that escaped through her half-opened door. When she emerged from her lair to get water at the fountain, with her waddling gait, head pushed forward, back hunched over, wrapped in a madras cloth, feet spread apart and horned toes gripping soil as if to maintain her balance, all the fights that were always starting up among the ill-mannered negroes would suddenly stop. The crowd scattered to let her draw her water. Some averted their gaze while others looked at her in a respectful way as if to say, "*Ouais*, Doudoute, *ou sé an mal fanm*, you are one bad-ass woman!"

Me, I looked at her and saw a certain sweetness. Her expression at times reflected something in the past, as if she could leave herself and travel to days, moments, or people from another time in her life, or maybe even further away. Also, I told myself that she could not be so evil after I had seen two little boys around her house who did not seem to fear her at all. One of them stuttered and was called Frantz. The other, who only came around from time to time, was called Jean-Luc and I think he was about my age. When I passed by, he looked at me in quite a bizarre way and one time when our eyes met he quickly ran to rejoin his brother as I if I had burned him with my gaze. They seemed very happy together, and I envied Frantz and Jean-Luc. Only the shrill voice of Doudoute seemed able to stop them. One time I saw Doudoute run after them with a stick, shouting, "Little scoundrels!" I later learned from Francelise, my school friend, that they had put a cat inside a boot and tossed it in the air several times before setting it on Doudoute's roof. The cat emerged in a daze, not dead yet because he had nine lives and this was only his fifth. But as the cat trembled, Frantz and Jean-Luc got scared not only about the beating of their lives they were about

Twist My Head, Make Me Cry!

to receive, but scared also of the cat, its feline gaze, its other lives, and its zombie powers. To earn its silence, they gave it one of the chicken legs that Doudoute had browned in a pot for the midday meal. When Doudoute caught them, she chased them around the house with that stick and I think their backsides are still echoing from the caning they got that day.

One time, I heard that Doudoute could make the living pass from one world to the next, and from one country to another. Interestingly, one of our neighbors whose daughter turned up pregnant at the age of thirteen went to see if they could benefit from her talents as a travel agent. Apparently, at the request of Doudoute, the mother dragged her daughter to Doudoute's house early one morning and the daughter never re-emerged. The mother returned to her house alone, crying from the bottom of her soul and beating her breast to the rhythmic chant of "Through my fault, through my fault, through my most grievous fault." Hoping to avoid the family's shame, Madame Désormais had pulled together her meager funds to send the daughter to stay with a second cousin in France. The women of the lakou shook their heads from right to left and sucked their teeth with a "tchiiip!" Their dried-up sunken cheeks blended with their high cheekbones and they said, *"Nonm'ay la té ka manjé gombo-la é tèt ay*—Her boyfriend was eating the little girl too! He was having the okra and the okra head too!"

When they arrived at Doudoute's, after a series of incantations that were unintelligible to the ears of mere mortals, Doudoute made the young girl stand up in the middle of the back room of her house. Surrounded by a cabalistic circle, with incantations of all sorts swirling around, there was a tin tub filled with blueish water that—without any assistance—rippled like it was being stirred by an offshore breeze. At the old woman's request, the young girl stepped over the bowl and disappeared into thin air, never to return . . . The same day she appeared in the bathroom of her cousin who

CAMILLE'S LAKOU

lived on the top floor of a seven-story walk-up apartment building in the eighteenth arrondissement of Paris in metropolitan France. It seems no one was surprised by this apparition.

Fetching Water

Shayé d'lo

MY MOTHER NEVER let me fetch the water. She was too scared of the numerous fights that broke out every day around the fountain. The neighborhood people had not yet mastered the art of forming a line, so it was very often that one found oneself the unwilling witness to an altercation that would turn physical. We never knew who had gotten there first and so the fountain became the place where many soap operas would play out along the canal water among the lakou folks. There, we learned everything about everyone, who was cheating on whom, or which young girl had gotten pregnant or been *dékaré*—raped—by nobody-knew-who. Of course, nobody really cared to know who had committed this act of violence against such a young girl. Apparently, she deserved it! She's the one who learned to walk like this or like that, like a nasty little . . . ! A little slut is what she is! In fact, all women were sluts. All they had to do was stay home! That was their place! If a young girl decided to leave the family house and *ba la ri chenn*—run the streets like a dog—she deserved everything that happened to her. She was looking for it. Actually, when we heard the women speaking, the neighborhood mothers, they would challenge each other in language that only the mothers of Monbruno Court understood. "My son is king in this barnyard! Too bad for those chicks that hang out behind the cage!"

In later years I finally understood. The same women who raised the girls also raised the boys! And according to my observations, boys had more freedom than girls, more right to enjoy themselves, to come and go when they pleased, touching girls there, where they were not supposed to, and even going further! All the girls had to do, for their part, was defend their virtue. In fact, it was their duty—and if they did not stick to it then they were just that—sluts, pure and simple! Me, I never wanted to be raped, nor did I want the neighborhood women to look at me like I was nasty. Later, as I got older, I would understand better what it was to be a young man in the lakou growing up with the idea of "doing something" for a woman . . . or for several . . .

At the fountain, we also learned which father slept with his own daughter and wound up getting her pregnant. That, however, was whispered very quietly while the young girl in question passed by with her eyes lowered. It was her fault after all! What gave her the idea to use the same towel as her father! The father himself was never questioned. The mother more often looked the other way and sided against her daughter. Not surprising that over time these young women mired themselves in madness or alcohol. Most of the ones who survived those two scourges became factories for children by different fathers. It was all like a well-orchestrated quadrille ball in which the men would take the lives of these women like a relay baton, and the price of a loaf of bread that soothed their hunger turned out to be another mouth to feed.

Mosquitos Don't Wanna Hear You Tell Them They're Skinny

Marengwen pa vlé tann di i mèg

BECAUSE MY MOTHER never wanted me to leave the house alone, I accompanied her on dozens of the round-trip journeys that she made from Monbruno Court to Fleret Court in order to keep the water barrel that we had behind the house full. Once the barrel was full, we had to cover it with a burlap cloth to keep leaves from the mango tree getting inside and messing it up. This way, we had water for several days to cook, bathe, and do laundry. There was a certain art to drawing this precious water. With a saucepan in my right hand, I had to fan the water with my left to avoid catching the tadpoles and mosquitos that grew in the barrel. This simple gesture with the back of the hand, caressing the surface of the water without touching it, made them scatter in the water like an upside-down explosion of fireworks and disappear for a time as if they had been swallowed up in the shadowy depths of the barrel. I focused, then, on drawing just the amount of water we needed for the moment but I had to do so without spilling a drop. That water was gold, so much so that Uncle Rifa who had set himself up in the garage that blocked our home from the main road, and kept us in the rear as if we were slaves, had running water in his garage. But he kept it locked up with a key when he wasn't there! *Ouais*, that water was really valuable! The few times each month when he was there, he watched us heading up and down the block "like dry beans boiling in a pot," without offering us even a single pail of water! All that was beyond the understanding of a seven-year-old girl. My mother said that when she became pregnant, my grandmother told her, "*Ou fè péché a'w, fè pénitans a'w*—You did the crime, now do the time!" and she refused to offer her any assistance. In fact, she kicked her out of the family house, and maybe that was her penance. By what miracle had we escaped malaria and the other maladies created to exterminate Black people? Only God could say . . . Wasn't it He who held the universe in his hands? We had to believe He had a plan. IbelieveinGodtheFatherAlmightyCreatorofHeavenandEarth . . . If He decided that our lot in life was to be born on this island of evil tongues, devoured by the cosmic gluttony of greedy Békés and white people from France, stuffed with empty promises and dreams of the mother land, mocked by the Syrians and Lebanese, and looked down on by the Malabar Indians, who was I to question Him? I had learned my catechism well! He had a plan . . . I had to believe there was a plan. My mother and I were still here, alive, planted firmly on our two feet as *négrès Gwadloup*. Those round-trip journeys to collect that precious water were the open book in which unfolded before my eyes, day after day, the life of the lakou. Each page of that book turned to the rhythm of our lives, our fights, and our quarrels. And, again, I wondered to myself . . .

60

Grab a Gadasammy!

Prengadassamy!

BEHIND OUR TWO-ROOM shack there was also a chicken coop. Once a year, my mother and I would travel to the docks in La Pointe to purchase chicks. When she had the means, we took a public bus, or T-A-G, that left from Raizet and dropped us downtown. The buses left us off at the entrance to the city center then went back to their departure terminal in the area around the new bridge behind Martenol. On their doors they carried the well-known names of Ramassamy, Moutousammy, Vingadasammy, and many-other-sammys and ran out to the most distant towns in Grande-Terre: Morne-à-l'Eau, Vieux Habitants, Petit Canal, Le Moule, Saint-François, all names that held a mysterious character for me. I imagined Vieux-Habitants full of *old* people, hunchbacked and bent over, walking with cane in hand and pipe in mouth, their faces cracked by years of suffering, ravaged by the erosion of life. In my child's mind, Petit-Canal was a different world where Black people drifted along on rickety boats, unable to set foot on dry land, condemned to carry on down a canal filled with floating debris, everything rotting, adrift in a rudderless ship of fate. Morne-à-l'Eau was a spring that flowed with fresh, clear water, but Black people were forbidden from accessing it. They were strictly limited to the pond water that cows used as watering holes. Le Moule was more familiar to me because my mother and her family came from that area. She had spoken to me of the beaches around the bay, and the other side of the island, and had promised to take me there one day. I could describe for you very well the coasts of France, Paris and its monuments, the Central Plateau, Joan of Arc, Rouen, etc., but Petit-Canal? I knew it not! That required imagination.

On the public buses, we always sat on benches covered in red or green vinyl that made our crotches sweat. Jammed in, one on top of another as if sharing a common destiny, we marinated in the heat and the smell of sweat trickling under armpits, covered by a forest of black and singed hair, squashed by colossally thick arms. I experienced these things while being whipped by the wind that blew in gusts through the interior of the bus, making me shed tears that left salt-water traces in the corner of my eyes as if I had spent the night crying out all the tears of my existence as a little Black girl from the lakou, with nappy hair, at the dawn of her life's journey.

The trip to La Pointe took forever, even though we only lived a few kilometers from downtown. The public buses stopped all the time. Even when a passenger boarded just thirty seconds before your destination, you made it a point to ask for the bus to stop exactly where you wanted to be let out. Not a second before or a second after. This entire operation was accomplished with a simple "Stop" or, in the nicer buses, with the help of a stop button. So there was an incessant commotion, a flowing in and flowing out movement that transformed the bus into a hungry beast that consumed an innumerable quantity of Black people throughout the day with gargantuan speed and ejected them out the back end of the bus in a uniquely scatological manner. Now that I think about it, I never saw a single white person, Béké, or even a mulatto using this type of bus. It was, to my eyes, reserved for all but the darkest Blacks.

Grab a Gadasammy!

Even a Malabar *kouli* would not risk it, except for the ones who drove the buses or worked as a driver's "aide."

Each bus had its own aide, a young man, very skinny and slim, generally a *ti zindiens* or "skinny little Indian" who posted up between the last row of seats and the rear door, which meant he had to be *really* thin! His role, apart from collecting the bus fare, was to guide or more often to shove the passengers toward the front of the bus while watching to make sure that all the seats were occupied. No space could be left empty, and these buses were always packed tight like a can of sardines. There was a constant and never-ending refrain of *"lévé, sizé—*get up, sit down" that accompanied those climbing on board and those getting off.

My sole pleasure on the public buses was the musical atmosphere that reigned there. Guadeloupean buses served as moving jukeboxes and contributed in their way to the Antillean hit parade. We heard all kinds of music: Guadeloupean beguines, Martinican mazurkas, salsa and meringue coming from the Spanish islands, konpa from Haiti, other Latin styles and cadence-lypsos from Dominica, and even more rhythms all blending into one another. This ambience created a pan-Caribbean atmosphere and gave us a feeling of brotherly union that broke down all linguistic barriers. We were all in the same boat and shared the same experience whether we were Haitian, Dominican, Puerto Rican, Cuban, Martinican, or Guadeloupean. In music, it really was a case of *"Menm biten, menm bagay—*Same show, different channel!"

Frébault Street

Lari Frébault

FROM THE MOMENT we arrived in La Pointe, we found ourselves assaulted from all sides by every kind of noise, with smells and colors that were rich and garish at the same time. The first thing we always saw were the *doukoune* or sweet snack vendors, seated on wooden stools at the corner of Frébault Street, who welcomed us with their refrain.

"*Doudou, chéri* . . . Sweets, cherie, I got the coconut ball candies with the pink head."

Their baskets were loaded with cakes, chopped and toasted coconut balls (including the pink-headed ones), golden *doucelettes* like caramel-fudge fondant, brown sticks of hard *sik doj* candy, sweet nougat bars with pistachio nuts, and of course my favorite: coconut lace.

Sadly, my pleasure there was always strictly visual. My mother would never stop in front of these merchants' displays. "Those people there don't know how to make cake!" she would say. "Also, you never know where their hands have been."

Then we would travel along Frébault Street looking to buy some freshly pressed cane juice, along with a spicy mackerel sandwich.

Frébault Street

There was always a line in front of the truck where they sold juice from tropical fruits, but no one ever seemed impatient. Everyone waited their turn for a chance to enjoy this nectar that seemed essential to an Antillean morning. The liquid was of an indeterminate color, shifting back and forth between brown and green bird poop, yet none of the customers seemed to find it repugnant. In later years, I understood the relation that existed between Black people and sugar cane. They extracted a certain pleasure from drinking the juice of their own labor, juice that had like them been pressed, crushed, reduced to pulp, and strained. Cane juice represented all that for a Guadeloupean. It was, as they said, a representation of the cycle of Antillean life. A Black man drank the juice that then became an integral part of his body, to be ejected later in secret (or not-so-secret) places as a natural fertilizer to nourish the traitorous cane.

I adored Frébault Street. Small and noisy, it gathered into itself the entirety of Guadeloupe. The people came from all over, from Basse-Terre, from Grande-Terre, and smaller villages and islands. There was every nuance of skin color from darkest black to palest *chabin*. From the skinniest flesh to the chubbiest. From hair like hard peppercorns to thin sprigs of chive. Their Kreyol was tinted with all sorts of different tonalities that made my mother say, "That one over there, that's a Capesterre man, that one!" or again, "Woy, papa! There goes another one straight from the plantation!" or yet again, "That one's from Basse-Terre people . . ." all said with an air of great confidence.

All these people came to La Pointe to buy shoes, fabric, and furniture while running all manner of errands. La Pointe was, then, the navel of Guadeloupe and because of its central location it attracted all her children from every corner of the island seeking refuge and sustenance. You could see stalls of shoemakers who spent all day long nailing and gluing back together shoes that had been gutted by children whose feet never stopped growing or by adult feet that had screamed for gnarled bunions and corns to be released from their painful leather confinement. With a little hammering, a row of tiny cobbler's nails was flattened into place and transformed the most mashed-up pair of brogans into decent shoes.

Toward the end of the street, a wide range of stores popped up on both sides offering everything for sale. There were off-the-rack clothes straight from Paris or Italy. There were Italian shoe stores and hardware stores, and most importantly, above all else, record stores where the men congregated like flies on honey. They came and listened to the latest hits and paid for them with their hard-earned, two-week paychecks without even flinching. The women carried the assault to the rest of the shops and in particular to the fabric stores. Buyers and sellers were worlds apart, but no one seemed to notice. Nevertheless, my little seven-year-old girl's eyes reflected images into my soul that would be permanently engraved in my memory. The images told me that each one had their place in this Guadeloupe of the 1960s. There was a place for Békés, a place for Lebanese or Syrians, a place for *kouli* Malabars, and a place for Blacks. No one, it seemed, cared to change the order of things. It had been decided at some point, by I don't know what greater authority, that the role of Black people was to ride on minibuses owned by Indians to go and spend the money they had earned painfully working for the white French man or on Béké lands in the stores of the Syrians and Lebanese. This is the way things were. And Black folks were content with that! It would never occur to them to question their place in the world. As the adults of Monbruno Court said, "After all, your real place is in the cemetery, *n'est-ce pas?*" No one was entitled to a place down here.

My mother followed her own triangular route that included Prisunic, the Saint-Antoine Market, and Market Place. She took great pleasure in handling the floral print fabrics that were spread out as far as the eye could see among the stalls of the Saint-Antoine

Frébault Street

Market. After a certain amount of time that to me seemed interminable, she bought three and half meters of fabric, a DMC spool of thread, decorative *à couvrir* buttons that she would cover with cloth, and some snap buttons that were more functional. At that moment, I knew she was planning to make me one of her latest fashion outfits and it was going to make me the laughing-stock of my classmates at school and among the lakou children. My mother had a chic style but it was always marred by bad cuts: the clothes she made for me always fit poorly on my small, skinny frame. Her necklines defied all the models for off-the-rack women's fashion from that period. I know now that she was ahead of her time—way, waaaay ahead, perhaps even too far ahead!

We went across the street to the Prisunic, next, to run more errands. The Prisunic was indeed a "unique" spot in La Pointe. To my knowledge it was the only place that had air conditioning. Because of that, there were many people who were positive that they would catch *cho é fwét*—fever and chills—there, and for them it was out of the question to set foot inside. I thought that my mother was very brave when she unflinchingly faced the wave of cold air that greeted her upon entering the store. Having parted this curtain of cold, we encountered another marvel of those times: the rolling steel escalator! It was fascinating, and you had to see it to believe the comic spectacle that unfolded at the foot of this great steel millipede that never stopped rising. The women in particular hesitated, put one foot forward, but never failed to execute a perfect split in spite of themselves. In the end, assisted by some charitable soul, they let themselves be dragged by the escalator, only to do the same dance at the top. My mother? She took me firmly by the hand and hopped! Just like that, we were off on our voyage to the top of Prisunic. We were going to check out all the provisions they had arrayed up there in a bric-a-brac jumble. All sorts of pots and pans, brooms, bedpans; everything was rubbing shoulders there without any shame. You could even find Gerflex mats coated with black tar bitumen we used to cover the planks of wood that made the floor back in our shack. The material was perfect. No need for glue to make it stick. Soon, however, the heat from the corrugated tin roof would melt the mat like wax candles in a church. While the floor was covered with rugs in garish shades of red, green, and yellow, holes had formed in the wooden planks from the humidity that chipped away at the ground under our feet just like the rats and cockroaches gnawed at our bread. The force of constantly walking across the floor had uncovered those holes like bloody scars, gaping wounds that the neighborhood rats and mice enjoyed using for their games of hide and seek.

On this particular day in La Pointe, we had purchased two young chickens, one that had all white down and the other with a rust-colored coat of feathers. I never chose black chickens. I named them Whitey and Carmelita, and I was in charge of giving them water and Purina baby chicken feed to eat in the morning and at night. It was a chore I carried out with no hesitation. Whitey and Carmelita were my children, my brothers and sisters, the unique spectators of my monologues and open-air theatrical shows. From behind the screen of their chicken coop, they had no other choice but to admire me and applaud me with their endless clucking.

A few steps away from their coop was the corner where our slop pail was enthroned. It was a green plastic bucket that received all the excrements from our little family, and it had to be emptied and cleaned every two days or so in the *tinette*, the lakou's communal toilet. Just as she did when it came to fetching water, my mother never sent me to *jeter le seau*, or empty the family chamber pot by myself. She said that only wicked stepmothers did such things and that she was certainly not one of those, not in that category at all. She was too afraid I would be viciously raped by one of the many scoundrels who were always hanging around there. Several times

Frébault Street

I witnessed fights between women who were quarrelling over the love or money of a man who had made empty promises to both of them. They found themselves around the community slop hole and suddenly the *tinette* became their stage and the bystanders there enjoyed a great time laughing at the misery of others free of charge. When that happened, my mother would hurry through her business and get out of there fast, pulling and dragging me at the same time, as if she knew we did not belong in that milieu. I saw this so many times and came to the conclusion that my mother was a beautiful apple mango that had landed mistakenly in a bag of rough, common, beefy mangoes with firm flesh.

If for one reason or another my mother did not have the time to empty the slop pail, which is to say the *contents* of the pail, it would become filled with tiny yellow creatures that swarmed and wriggled all over the place, climbing up the pail on all sides, covering the face of the lid while trying to escape and finally transforming themselves into *yenyen* or flies that quickly landed on a neighbor's piece of well-roasted meat, or a piece of dried bread held by a child in the next house over, or perhaps even on mine . . . With a lazy swipe of my hand, I would brush them away and continue to eat my bread with no quivering in my body or quaking in my heart. Who knew what tomorrow would bring? Might as well continue eating my bread. Those flies had their affairs and I had mine.

I was one year older than my cousin, Jean-Luc. We did everything together, even doing our business together in the family's poop bucket (though this is unthinkable now). I remember this was during the time when Tante Carmelita and her children, my cousins, all lived with us in Monbruno Court. As if by magic, we always wanted to go on the pail at the same time. The problem was we only had one bucket for slops, which was a white earthenware container with a blue rim, installed at the end of the yard, behind the house under the mango tree. We would both sit on the pail,

69

each one leaning against the other's back, and there we would stay, singing and chatting and sharing our little secrets. The important thing was to finish at the same time or one would have to wait for the other before getting up.

"*Ou ja fini*—You done?"

"No, wait for me, I'm not done yet."

One day, however, and it was not a good day at all, the inevitable happened. Much like any other day, we sat on the toilet while our other cousins played hide and seek around us, oblivious to the foul smells wafting up from below our butts. It was an odor we accepted in the same way we accepted the smell of the earth after it rains, the smell of June plum in the air, or again the smell of thousands of rotten mangos lying on the ground under the tree invaded by hordes of no-see-ums, what we called *yenyen* flies, or the smell of carrion along the roadside that stayed there for days liquifying under the hot Guadeloupean sun, gradually eaten by worms and other scavengers. On this particular day, I don't know what *ladjablès* devil caused me to get up before Jean-Luc, as this had never happened before. Pushed by some invisible spring, I hopped off the pail with a single leap and . . . shoop-boom! Jean-Luc landed in the poop pail, folded in half with his legs in the air and his arms flapping uselessly as he tried in vain to get out. The cousins came running to admire up close the scatological spectacle now displayed before our eyes. Jean-Luc was covered from head to foot in excrement, dripping and stinking, crying, screaming, and jumping around amid the laughter of the others who stood there giggling. When I think about it, at that very moment I had before me the perfect representation of our existence in Monbruno Court, and perhaps even of our future and especially that of Jean-Luc.

Our mothers came running quickly, alerted by the heckling that something had transpired that was not really kosher. Soon, armed with a bucket of water, soap, and medicinal plants, Tante Carmelita

Frébault Street

took care of Jean-Luc and my mother saw to my backside. It was our last time on the outhouse toilet together in a *caca à deux*, and our relationship would never be the same.

"Those People . . ."

Sé kalité moun la sa!

THIS WAS THE TIME when all the family, at least the family I knew, still lived together: Grandmother, Tante Carmelita, my cousins Maryse, Christian, Jean-Luc, and Eddie, my mother, and me. In those times, the only image we had of an adult male was Uncle Richard, who had not yet appropriated all the land where the family house sat on its four cinder blocks. He had not yet had the opportunity to reveal himself for what he truly was: a greedy miser of the worst kind, an *agoulou granfal as we said in Kreyol.*

I have only vague memories of my childhood house, but we all slept together pell-mell among our rags after having taken turns washing up in a green plastic tureen. Though we lived in poverty, our parents saw it as their duty to insist on cleanliness. In fact, we didn't have anything *but* that cleanliness. Every morning began with an obligatory toilette, and in the afternoon another washing, and at night we never forgot to wash our feet before going to bed. At least once a week there was a serious scrub-down. My mother or grandmother loved to scour our bodies with leaves that had mystical scents. They took great care visiting nearby thickets to gather

"Those People . . ."

various shrubs that were chosen by virtue of their benefits: vetiver, wild ferns, and basil, some plant with analgesic and anti-bacterial properties, and soursop leaves that were good for insomnia. These were soaked overnight in a cast iron. After the leaves were left to cook all day in the hot sun, I suppose in order to absorb celestial blessings, the adults grabbed us one after the other and soaked us in the water, which had taken on a coffee color. Then they began to rub our bodies with all their force, almost slaying our skin in the process, and it went on for a period of time that to me seemed infinite. It was literally as if they wanted to scrub the blackness off of us, and we heard their interjections, like, "Chile, do you really wanna *make* me do this again?" or "Where in the *world* did *this* scratch come from?"

In fact, this was a way for them to examine us closely and reassure themselves that we had not picked up anything that was not strictly Christian, any malady that could have come from sorcery caused by Madame So-and-So. According to them, these herbal baths had magical benefits and protected us against malign spirits and most of all against the evil works of Miss Whomever, who more than anything else wanted us to fail in life. By the way it was she who had made Tante Carmélita's feet crack open everywhere, something no doctor had been able to explain or cure. It was this same Madame Whatsits who made it so that mother had one foot smaller than the other and always had foot problems. My mother herself told me how, one day, for an unknown reason, that woman had poured some whitish water in front of our door and my mother had inadvertently stepped in it. Her foot then became twisted into the shape of a horse's hoof and she had to make all sorts of pilgrimages to find a cure. Because of all that, I was subsequently forbidden to walk on Miss Unmentionable's sidewalk and above all I was never to look her in the eye.

My cousins and I entertained ourselves in the morning by telling each other our dreams. As for dreams, I never had any. I was never able to remember what had happened to me during the night. So I invented stories and dreamed my dreams out loud. They were just gibberish really, and my cousins mocked me. One day I told them that I had dreamt of a car running over my stomach. That did not seem convincing to them, and like always, they mocked me. This meant that very often I felt alone among them. I watched them grow up around me without understanding what separated us. They argued, they fought, they reconciled. It was not like that between them and me. There always seemed to be an invisible film that separated without truly dividing us. During the long school holidays, their mother sent them to Le Moule, the city of her childhood where they spent all their long vacations. Needless to say, after their departure the sun went down and the moon forgot to rise in Monbruno Court until the end of the school holidays. They came back from Le Moule, were all the time talking among themselves and sharing stories of their adventures in Portland, Le Moule, of beaches, and cattle watering holes. Me, I never had anything to share. There was a line between us that I could never quite define. I felt that, for them, I was the cousin to whom nothing ever happened, who never had anything to tell. Their eyes opened up a window for me on the outside world beyond Monbruno Court.

At this age, for me everything was a marvel. This was especially true when it came to lights. There was no electricity where we lived so every night our parents lit a gas lamp that had to be filled with kerosene. When I think about it, we all could have been burned alive or poisoned by noxious fumes from that lamp, but the only thing it seemed to do, oddly enough, was to cause Eddie to always wake up with his nostrils full of oily smoke residue. The lamp was made up of a round reservoir set on a base-plate, a glass collar that resembled a queen's crown and from which emerged a felt-tongue wick soaked in the blue liquid our parents had poured into the reservoir.

"Those People . . ."

Once the wick was lit, we placed a cylindrical lamp glass between the teeth of the crown after taking great care to clean the glass so there was no trace of smudges. Then a sputtering light emerged, haloed with a blueish crown and from which arose a spiral of black smoke, like a snake being charmed by some invisible flute player. That same smoke was going to deposit itself like a film on the walls of the lamp glass, and later would find itself lodged in Eddie's nostrils. Who knows, maybe that was the cause of all the mucus that bit by bit had made its way almost to his brain, deposited there like a film that kept Eddie trapped in an existence as dull as the light coming out of the gas lamp . . . who knows?

The lamplight projected a strange reality on us. Our reality. When we were seated around the table, a curious dance played out in our eyes. Little sparks were reflected in the blacks of our eyes and flickered in a way that made us seem like *clindindins*, or fireflies. When we came near the lamp, our faces took on a golden tint that vanished as soon as we moved away from the only source of illumination. Very quickly, we then became shadows without form like zombies preparing for their nocturnal dance. At that point, only our eyes and our very white teeth appeared in the shadow and seemed to form a chain of cowrie shells suspended in the air by the invisible wings of luminous *clindindins*.

If someone needed to go from one room to the next, they had to take the lamp with them, leaving the others in the deepest obscurity, but the place was immediately studded with little stars that smiled at us through holes drilled in our tin roof. Or they would simply lift up the lamp glass with one hand using a towel, and with the other hand tilt a candle toward the flame in order to light it and in the process avoid wasting another match. The candle then became another source of light and would soon find its bottom glued to a table or dresser by its own wax, thereby illuminating the existence of another negro with no future. Pitiful was the light, and pitiful was the existence of both the candle and we, the wretched souls of Monbruno Court.

In Monbruno Court, which had lately been rechristened as "Sailors' Bridge Court," night came on very fast. And with the night came storytelling time and the tales told to us by our elders, Maryse and Christian. Maryse's stories were the most interesting ones. She had such an ability to breathe life into her characters, imitating their voices, their gestures, their body movements, that we often fell asleep to a volley of tears and screaming, huddled together with our eyelids shut tight out of fear that the *ladjablès* demon would find us during her nocturnal visits among the little children.

And so night came. After dining on a meager soup, hot cocoa without milk, and stale bread, we took great care rinsing our mouths out with water. Bad luck to the boy or girl who forgot or neglected this most important ritual. He or she would then hear: "Who didn't swish water in their mouth? What kind of nasty *malpwop* mess are you? Go on, get that water in your mouth, you nasty *malpwop*!" All that was washed down with a slap on the back of the head that made you fly from one end of the small room to the other. Seemingly by chance, this type of incident happened to Eddie most often and only occasionally to Jean-Luc. Although this hygiene might have left a lot to be desired, we all had very white and very healthy teeth and on top of that none of my cousins had even a single cavity. I recall one time in second grade, I think, that Mme. Cesaire chose me as an example to the other students of what it meant to have molars that were healthy and white. It was like we had discovered the secret of very white teeth. Maryse had shown me that by rubbing a nice piece of charcoal on your teeth and gums you could ensure very good dental health. I think she was right since years later in France, when I was in my last year of college, a classmate asked me the following question: "Why are your teeth so white and mine so yellow?" and then added "No doubt it's because of the contrast

"Those People . . ."

with your skin." In response, I could only smile, proud that I had such white teeth.

Then, after we had rinsed out our mouths, we set up our bedding, a bundle of rags in a corner of the space that served as dining room, living room, bedroom, and utility room. These rags had spent the day in the sun hanging on the corrugated tin barrier that separated our house from Mme. Coquin's. The sun seemed to have the power to kill all the piss smells and all the vermin that had the misfortune to have taken up free lodging in our miserable filth during the night. Those rags also represented our family history. There, we could find baby booties, panties and underwear with holes in them, and shirts that had been rubbed against the dirty backs of each and every one of us, from the biggest to the smallest, to finally end up drowned in our daily piss or torn into strips that we used to wipe our backsides for lack of toilet paper. If we looked closely, we could find clothes there that had belonged to our parents, to Tante Emile, or to Tante Amour Filial. Those were our favorite discoveries. The clothes from these two aunts stood out from the rest, just like a gamecock among hens in a barnyard. It was all glitter, bright sparkles, full support bras and sexy panties, evidence of a life that was very different from our own. These aunts were the two youngest in the family and had detached themselves very quickly from our world, but their clothes told us stories about the life they led. From the hair salon where they hung out around the local Békés and poor whites from the countryside, they looked at us from on high, saying "Those people . . ." with an air that was so disdainful you would have said they were offended by the magnitude of the poverty that surrounded us. So we invented stories: they were the fruit of our imagination or simply snippets of conversation overheard from the adults during the day and performed by us and for us on stage in the theatre we made from our tent of rags.

CAMILLE'S LAKOU

Those rags felt like the sweetness of a grandmother's caress, the warmth of our mothers' arms, the roughness and coldness of a day with neither bread nor meat.

So we sat around our oldest cousin, Maryse, and if by chance no fights had broken out among us, no punch had been landed on Eddie's nose, we would listen to Maryse until our tired eyelids fell down over the heavy seeds of our eyeballs and one by one we slumped down on our makeshift bed. For us, this was our world, our childhood nights as lakou people.

Mornings always began with the same refrain: "Who pissed on me!" It was almost impossible to find the culprit who, in the darkest depths of night, had found the means to change into some makeshift items found in the rags during the night. That was one of the benefits of sleeping on rags, though: we had our own wardrobe for all occasions!

Eventually, my cousins had to leave. Tante Carmélita took up with Bardo and they found a house in Carmont Court, the lakou across from ours. I found myself alone again, without brother, without sister, without cousins, without anyone to liven up my existence. To add to my misery, my Uncle Richard, or TonTon Rifa as I called him, had decided to take half the family house to set himself up in another neighborhood with his new wife. I say "new" because he had spent several years living with a different Black woman from the neighborhood. She had given him three beautiful children, cousins whom I dearly loved but who lived far from the lakou. TonTon had left her to go live with a smooth-haired *chabine* who worked in the general hospital. I never understood what had attracted him to this woman who had nothing but contempt for the entire family. She looked us over from top to bottom, stared at us, and mouthed a tepid "bonjour" to grandmother. Apart from the color of her skin and her clear blue eyes that appeared to give her certain privileges in our society, I found nothing about her to be at all attractive. Actually, I

78

"Those People . . ."

was scared of her. When I went to visit my uncle, she received me on the veranda. She never invited me to come inside. I much preferred my Tante Mercedes, a hardworking woman who ruled her family by barking out orders. Her children followed her pointed fingers and glances obediently. And woe unto me if I had not made up the bed or cleaned up my dish. She scolded me in her screaming voice that often made me tremble in fear. Nevertheless, I knew she was sincere and had a good heart. What's more, she made the best court-bouillon in the area. She kept a good house and did not shy away from work. In my eyes, she was a fine, upstanding woman who did not need a man to do anything for her!

How You Doing, Baby Girl?

Ka'a sa pitit a manman?

FROM TIME TO TIME, my other cousins, Vivianne, Richard, and Coline, visited us. Tante Amour (not Tante Amour Filial, who recently had been rebaptized as "Annette," and one could only wonder why) had moved away from the family to go live with her man in another neighborhood I did not know very well. We only visited her rarely and for obvious reasons. Her house was filthy, like the mouths of her children. Everything was covered in dirt and dust, and the ground merged with the mud that surrounded the house. From the bits of conversation I was able to catch between my mother and her older sister, I gathered that Uncle Cléonte, who was the father not of Vivianne but of Richard and Coline, had put her through every kind of misery. He beat her through and through! His head was always enveloped in the vapors of the world of Karukéra rum from which he only emerged to beat her over and over again! Assaulted by asthma attacks that plunged her into an epileptic fit more often than not, unable to find a job with children pulling on her skirts from all sides, Tante Amour wasted away in this misery. Elena, her

How You Doing, Baby Girl?

oldest daughter (I think she actually was Cléonte's child), escaped early on from this milieu and only visited rarely. So my aunt found herself alone. Alone with her precarious health, her Cléonte, and her gang of unleashed brats. Regardless, all those children there were like a three-headed centipede, wriggling like little worms, nonstop shouting, jumping, observing, and swearing at each other while Tante Amour sat there without saying a word, as if she were somewhere else and these scenes did not concern her. She had the power to escape her reality while still remaining in her house, seated, her gaze fixed on an invisible point in space somewhere right there in the confines of her shack. The children were left to their own devices and grew like weeds. Mother never allowed me to spend any days there with those cousins. I never went to their house except with her, and she only ever stayed there for a few minutes. Yet my mother adored her older sister even if she never understood why their mother chose to bypass Monbruno Court without ever stopping off even briefly at our house on her way to visit Amour in the neighborhood around the Sanitation Department. That was one cause of her pain. She talked about it all the time with her man, who always advised her to forget about her mother and stop talking to her. These conversations, which I heard from the other side of a multicolored slatted curtain that separated my mother's room from the small all-purpose chamber where I slept in my rags on the floor, caused me a lot of pain because I adored my grandmother. She was the only person who, sitting me on her lap, knew how to say exactly the right words to warm my little Black body with its nappy head: "How you doing, baby girl! *Ka'a sa pitit a maman!*" I snuggled up in her arms, buried my face in her neck the better to take in her smoky scent, and I knew then what it was to be loved. That smell of burnt wood charcoal signified for me this country of Guadeloupe that seemed so big to me. It was a comforting perfume that reminded me of my grandmother's caresses and made me feel

CAMILLE'S LAKOU

that everything down here was going to be fine. Anywhere I went and smelled that charcoal bonfire smell, I knew then that I loved my island and that she loved me in return.

My grandmother's touch and those few words that she said only to me made me feel that this life was worth the pain of living it. She was beautiful, my grandmother. The skin on her face was yam-colored, and soft like the skin of a passion fruit. It was well-drawn, smooth, wrinkle-free, and defined by piercing little eyes that seemed to know everything that was happening in your heart. I don't remember her mouth, I think because my gaze always landed on her cheekbones. They were high. It was as if she had stuck a malacca apple on each side of her face, wedged in between her teeth and the inside of her cheeks. Those cheekbones gave her face a very sculpted "V" shape, as if she had been delicately carved out of a nice piece of ebony wood. She wore her ash-colored braids piled up on her head in a crown. When she took them down, they fell around her shoulders and Grandmother was proud to remind us that she came from a beautiful race of Black people, a Black Kalinago Carib! Later on, in going through my schoolbooks, I thought I saw the resemblance between her and Carib Indians, the man-eating barbarians of whom the teacher had spoken (briefly). In fact, I think that's all I learned about those so-called Indians, those man-eating barbarians. I had a hard time understanding the relationship between them and my grandmother, who was a hardworking woman, very gentle and very proud of her race.

Grandmother had moved in with Kolo. Let's say rather that she shared the house and maybe her bedroom with this little old man. He was thin and a bit hunchbacked, with a lower lip that hung down excessively and exposed the tendons connecting his lip to his jaw. In fact, she never declared that Kolo was her man. She said, "He's a cousin of mine." Her daughters would explode with laughter at that and respond with a long "kip" or "stupes." "*Sé sa! Kouzen koté kuys!*" they would say, "More like kissin cousins!" and punctuate it by sharing a look of complicity between them. I never really knew if Kolo was her man or her cousin. Still they got along very well with each other and had a good life. Me, I was a little afraid of him because he always had a stick in his hand that he chased my cousins and me with, crying "*Krazé bwa!* Get the hell out of here!" while brandishing this stick and swinging it over our heads. And we, we would scatter throughout the house knocking things over like stampeding elephants crushing trees in a forest. Eventually, we would find each other, with great bursts of laughter from the oldest and great trembling from me, hiding further away in the savannah behind my grandmother's house. Kolo used this cane like a third leg because he had a little trouble getting around.

Grandmother and he lived in this two-room shack with a chicken cage and a rabbit pen in the back. I loved visiting my grandmother and sometimes my mother left me for hours at her house or at Tante Carmélita's who lived close by in another two-room place. She even let me stay there overnight once or twice. I never understood why my Cousin Maryse harbored such hatred for Bardo, her stepfather and husband of Tante Carmélita. Bardo had agreed to move in with my aunt and tolerated the four outside children she had inherited from a previous dad who never took care of them. He would later give her three more. I do believe that Maryse, in the fullness of her fifteen years, was very special to him and he allowed himself to be "comfortable" with her. She was always on guard when he was around, and they were always quarrelling. No, no, no, that relationship was not very *Catholique*! As soon as she got a chance to get out of that house, she quickly found herself pregnant and went to live with the father of her child in his family home in Sainte-Rose, clearly repeating a cycle that imprisoned the women and families of Guadeloupe. Was that what was waiting for me, too? Would I have to find a man to take care of me while giving me as many children as he wanted (because that was his "strength")? The power of men was in the fruit of their loins, and they made sure to sow their seed to the four winds. The Guadeloupean man was like a great big Larousse dictionary with its saying "*Je sème à tous vents*" that defined the meaning of life for Guadeloupean women, though not with words fixed on a page. Without him, they were nothing! I understood, then, that the duty of women was to please their men, and that they should make sure to find one at all costs and at a very young age. It didn't matter if he was married! Besides, what did a name really mean if a woman couldn't keep her man? "*Pran kouraj mafi,*" the older women would say, "Take heart my girl, you will find a man to take care of you, *ou ké trouvé on nonm ki ké fè on biten ba'w!*" I firmly believe that this is where our fear and shame come from. What if I couldn't find a man? What would become of me then? Misery? Death? Shame? And again I wondered . . .

From those visits to my aunt, I understood very well the man's place in a home. Bardo always got the best cuts when it came to chicken or anything else. Apparently, he liked thighs the most and that was his favorite piece. For me, the wing was the best because it really soaked up the flavor of any seasoning, plus I never had to fight anyone over a thigh. The man was always served first with the best pieces arrayed on his plate. Kids, they didn't need much. Some rice and a little sauce did the trick. A piece of yam with the sauce from a fish was plenty! At dinner time, all my cousins would assault their mother, trying to extract a piece of chicken from her, or the end of a fishtail, or even the head. Ahhhh, the head! How many tasty treasures were buried in that fish head! It required a certain artistry to enjoy the flavors while taking great care to avoid the many pitfalls that lay in wait for the novice diner. Everywhere there were bones that needed to be sucked. Big and small, the cousins all surrounded her just like little chicks with their mouths wide open, waiting for the little leftover morsels that their mother

How You Doing, Baby Girl?

had saved for them. Then, surrendering to their onslaught, she would take a small piece of fish, grilled meat, or other food out of her mouth and gave each one a bite, "*Mi, mi, mi, mi, mi! Pa vin anko!* Here, here, here you go! Don't come back for more!" This spectacle was repeated whenever I spent time with my cousins. I always remained on the sidelines, an incredulous witness to these scenes from my cousins' daily life. At least at my mother's, when there was meat on the table I got the biggest piece, though it must be said that there were only three of us in the household—my step-father, my mother, and me.

So, every morning, Tante Carmelita was busy in the kitchen. After peeling the white or yellow yams, the sweet potatoes and ripe maduro plantains, she put them in a black cast iron cooking pot and covered them in water. She would then add coarse salt that she carefully measured in the palm of her hand. For this, she put her hand in the shape of a small bowl. She could tell just by looking at it if the measure was correct or not. It was the same with us. We used our palms to measure sugar as well as salt. It was perfect! So, once she had put the ground provisions over the flame on her little two-burner gas stove, she began making the fish court-bouillon. She was doing great. She asked us to chop of the chives that Maryse had cut into very thin strips, along with some finely minced parsley. Next, we peeled the garlic and this all happened while the boys, Eddie and Jean-Luc, were outside chasing lizards, but to me that hardly mattered. I loved the smell of the spices and anyway I was not very friendly with the lizards who always threatened me by pushing their throats out like a knife thrust as soon as I approached. In any case, without tasting the sauce, I knew the court-bouillon stew would be delicious. Who knew, maybe that day would be our lucky day and we would get the fish head. Of all the parts of the head, I believe I most preferred the brains. They were hidden, imprisoned in a labyrinth of small bones with thousands of tiny caverns. Each one contained a soft, marrow-like substance that had a particular taste of earth combined with the spicy taste of the stew. Our task was to pull very hard by sucking through our mouth and repeating small contractions of our little tongues in order to dislodge this delectable brain marrow that had been soaked in the seasoning of the court-bouillon. Another part of the head that we loved to suck on was the eye! The fish eyes were each wrapped in a bubble of viscous fluid intended, I think, to protect the eye. Inside this bubble was the fish's *koko zié*, or eyeball, that resembled a small seed. It was both hard and soft at the same time and we chewed on it until it popped out of its protective fluid casing. Once separated from the membrane that surrounded them, we would spit the eyeballs out from our mouths and the boys enjoyed playing marbles with them. The mix of bigmouth fish, catfish, and other types of red and blue fish that Tante Carmelita had placed on a bed of chives, garlic, parsley, and thyme, before sautéing it to perfection in a *bè wouj* achiote roux with a little Alba oil, gave a delicious flavor to this stew in which we would soon be dipping our piece of yam or potato. When the cooking was almost done, she added fresh crushed tomatoes, juice from a lime, and another garlic clove. She covered the lid of the sauté pan but not before throwing in the *Bonda-Man-Jak* pepper! This part only lasted a few minutes, hence the name "court," or "fast" bouillon. Woe unto us, though, if we inadvertently bit into a piece of the pepper, which often was the same color as the tomatoes. When that happened, what followed was screaming, crying, and drooling until that stinging heat subsided or disappeared. The effects of the pepper were identical to biting ants that only attacked after they had silently climbed up onto your foot and at the command of their captain all stung at the same time. Then you screamed, cried, danced, and drooled while rubbing and scratching your foot and wondering, How they could have gotten all over you without you noticing? The *Bonda-Man-Jak* pepper was exactly like that!

How You Doing, Baby Girl?

Sometimes, the yams and sweet plantains were replaced with green banana and slices of breadfruit. It was impossible to get Maryse to swallow the breadfruit though Tante Carmelita tried to do it all the time. These scenes between my cousin and her mother were funny and sad at the same time. Sad because it always ended with a beating for Maryse, who screamed and cried out all the tears inside her, but funny because Tante Carmelita would chase after her, running all throughout the house until she could grab her by her golden *chabine* hair.

At least Maryse had some hair to pull, it must be said, unlike me, whose little braids did not even reach to my ears. Her hair was long and stood up on her head. Every day, my aunt had to do her hair. She sat Maryse down between her legs and armed with a fine-toothed comb she fought and pulled on her hair until she could untangle and tame it into two plaits that fell over her shoulders. And Maryse would cry and scream as we laughed and encouraged her while we waited for this daily spectacle to end. She was not the only one to suffer through this torture on a daily basis. All the young girls in the neighboring yards were screaming and crying before school. Mine was short, so the ordeal was over quickly, but those whose hair was kinky and longer would be cursed by their mothers for having peppercorn beads on their head. If they were unfortunate enough to move their head in the wrong direction, or if they simply tried to escape the torture, they were hit repeatedly with the same comb that bit into their hair. And me, I wondered, Why? Really, though, why were things like this?

87

Catholic Church

L'église catholique

OUR-FATHER-WHO-ART-IN-HEAVEN-HALLOWED-BE-THY-
NAME.

The only thing I really remember of the Catholic church is the vendors that lined up outside the exit of Saints Peter and Paul Church, where they sold us their little treasures of coconut lace or *dentelles*, cakes, and fudge. The *dentelles* were my favorite: baked to golden perfection in smooth, flat sheets, very fine and very sweet, these candies were the highlight of my Sundays. I really think that, except for them, I would never have gone to church at all.

Sacré-Coeur Church was, from my child's perspective, the most imposing and massive building in this section of La Pointe. Its high walls were coated with a grey residue of sea salt and they stretched up to a small tower that held the biggest bell I had ever seen in all my seven years. For me and all the La Pointe-dwellers, this bell sounded out the rhythm of our days just as much as the roosters that crowed their *kokiyoko* in all the nearby yards.

The interior of the church intimidated me. It was dark inside and smelled of fading candle wax mixed with mothballs and the stench of stale piss—*pisa koronpi*—emanating from the church's

Catholic Church

many hidden corners. The negros of that era were famous for their bad manners. They saw no problem in relieving themselves when- and wherever the urge overtook them. It was also very common to see a mother helping her child to squat in a corner . . . It was . . . natural! In fact, I cannot remember seeing a single toilet anywhere in that church, nor in any public buildings for that matter.

The church pews were a dark shade that reminded me of the color of coffins. They were made of some hardwood that, when touched, revealed centuries-old indentations made by the fingers of thousands of negros who, over the years, came there seeking refuge, an answer to their prayers addressed to God Himself or one of his many saints, or even to the gods who were not supposed to frequent this particular holy place. During the week, all those who met there maintained the same posture. Most of the time they were little old women with hunched backs and shifty eyes. In fact, I don't remember ever seeing a man there, except on Sunday mornings. Sometimes, there were one or two mothers crying silent tears, kneeling before the altar or making the sign of the cross and genuflecting. My mother was in this category. I had to accompany her and follow her during her pilgrimage between the statues of all the other saints like Saint Michael or Saint Anthony of Padua, all of them gazing down upon our misery. However, none of them had ever raised even a single hand to ease our misery. Day after day, I ate the same red rice, breadfruit, white dumplings, or dumpling and red beans, and all without any smoked pig's tail or bacon!

I wondered what the priest did during the day. We never actu- ally saw him except during the daily masses at five or six o'clock and the one on Sunday morning. Where did he go the rest of the time? What did he do? That was a pure mystery to me! I know that the back door of the church was where "the devil married his daughter," which is also what we said when there were sunbeams shining during rainy weather. The door opened from time to time for exchanges between little veiled women, dressed all in blue or all in white. They say that he sold them holy water . . . They also say that Mirna's little girl had eyes that sparkled the same shade of blue as Father's. They even added, crossing themselves quickly, that this child had not grown in Mirna's womb through the workings of the Holy Spirit and that it was, rather, the result of her numerous visits to the confessional. Others swore they had seen Monsieur l'Abbé come out through the same back door where he was no doubt going to join Mirna or perhaps another of his little sapotille brown-skinned fantasies in the backstreets of La Pointe! Anyway, no one knows how exactly Mirna came to have this child with amber skin and silken hair, but that baby was always pampered by everyone! Everyone stroked her smooth hair and loudly exclaimed how pretty she was. Nobody bothered to look at Nadine, Mirna's first daughter, also from an unknown father. She was barely a year older than her little sister. She had almond-shaped eyes that shone like fireflies and skin the color of ebony. No one noticed her. She was, as it were, invisible. She remained seated at the front door, right next to the basket in which her little sister slept, protecting her from the onslaught of flies that were thirsty for the sweetness of her brand-new baby skin. And me, as I passed by their shack with my mother, I wondered . . .

However, the smell of mothballs from Sunday dresses and the smell of sugared almonds and other sweets still lingers in my memories of Saints Peter and Paul Church, or the Sacré-Coeur Church, where mother sent me every Sunday. She didn't go herself, but woe to me if I dared to refuse this chore. In church, I always sat in the last rows where I could hardly hear the priest's litanies. That way, I could tell the truth to my mother when I had to answer the eternal question:

"*Ka labé la di?* What'd the priest say?"

"I never understand what Monsieur l'Abbé says. He's a new priest

Catholic Church

and he talks too fast." With that, she left me alone and returned to her regular Sunday routine . . . Vegetable soup.

"Through my fault, through my fault, through my most grievous fault, I ask Blessed Mary ever-Virgin . . ." I always asked myself what was that great fault that all the Blacks of Guadeloupe had committed to find themselves kneeling every Sunday, surrounded by these cold, white statues with bulging eyes that watched us without seeing us. Why did we have to kiss their feet? What could they do for us, imprisoned on their pedestals of cold marble? They were fixed there, Sunday after Sunday. And Sunday after Sunday the same people marched up to their feet, repeatedly striking their chests. Those same faithful moved quickly to the back of the church to shake hands with the same priest who had just delivered a sermon about serving the Good Lord Jesus, to buy holy water purchased for a good price in order to put a butt-busting *fann tchou* hex on the neighbor who had dared to expand or improve their house, or to tie up a baby in the belly of the husband's mistress because never would she give birth to a bastard who would take bread from the mouths of legitimate children, or to secure work in a government job, or to help a nephew successfully pass an exam, or again to *maré* or tie up that young man who was courting their daughter and whose intentions were unknown. So, before he could rent space in her womb on credit, or before the Holy Spirit could conduct an operation on her, they had to block the gentleman with conjure. I saw all that, I heard all that. And I wondered . . .

All these observations were bouncing around in my head and no one could give me an answer to the questions that troubled me. This scene that included the white priest with blue eyes, the mother superior and the nuns with white skin, blond hair, and ruthless mien, the Blacks kneeling at the feet of these statues covered in fly shit or opening their mouths big enough to swallow up the white body of Christ seemed normal to everyone. The Hail Marys, the Credos and

Our Fathers, seemed to block the impact of *gadèdzafè* charms, *sosyé* witchcraft, and *pisa koronpi* that had been tossed the night before just in front of the neighbor's door, not to mention the little black dolls wrapped in a jute bag and left at the crossroads. You had to be really careful not to step on them for fear of attracting a *gwopié* swollen foot curse. This is surely what had happened to Lorna, our neighbor who lived two houses up in the lakou. She came and went day after day, dragging a foot as big as a magpie and as deformed as an eddo. Yet didn't she go to church every Sunday and even on certain days of the week?

On Wednesdays, the Catholic church was still given over to catechism, the endless repetition of "Hail-Mary-Full-of-Grace" (or "grease" depending on your sense humor), the "I-believe-in-God-the-Father-Almighty" and not forgetting the "Our-Father-who-art-in-Heaven" along with many other prayers and religious devotions that escape me now.

Around the age of nine years old, I went through another religious experience. My grandmother took me with her to a small evangelical church that had just opened in Raizet. The experience transported me to a different world. A world where the faithful had, so to speak, a personal relationship with the Good Lord. He Himself remained invisible at all times but the energy released in these encounters between the brothers and sisters (as they all called each other) was palpable and contagious. I fell in love with this new atmosphere, these songs, these religious hymns and this feeling of fraternity that seemed to unite all the faithful. So I accompanied my grandmother to this church for some time until the day she decided not to go there anymore, following a little misunderstanding between her and Sister Tazi. Apparently, she herself and the entire church (some twenty members) insisted that grandmother ask forgiveness for some obscure offense she had committed against Sister Tazi. Like the good fighting Caribbean matadora she was, my grandmother had refused to participate in this exercise, proclaiming that she had nothing to reproach herself for and that she was certainly not going to let herself be led by anyone like that. With that, she turned on her heels and left the church, never to set foot there again.

As for me, I didn't understand the business of these grown women and I was angry with my grandmother for no longer taking me to church with her. Bored by the idea that the church in Pointe-à-Pitre was going to remain my only place of salvation, I therefore resigned myself and continued this chore that was repeated every Sunday morning. Soon, however, guided by I don't know what spirit, I took hold of my mother's Bible that lay covered with a layer of dust under her bed, on a board that rested on two blocks of cement and served, with three other boards, as a bedframe. With this Bible, my mother had taught me to read. It was the only reminder of my linguistic fights with Nebuchadnezzar, the only trophy in my library at the time, apart of course from the numerous *Nous-Deux*, *Ombrax*, and *Lucky Luke* pulp magazines that I stole from my stepfather, and that Bible transported me to another world. The story of Adam and Eve fascinated me. I had trouble reconciling the fact that the image I had of these two individuals in my young-girl-with-the-nappy-head mind did not correspond in any way to the image I had seen in so many church pamphlets. Even later, when I was twelve years old and had finally obtained permission from my mother to leave the Catholic Church in order to be able to attend the Evangelical Church of Guadeloupe, in all our tracts that were distributed to all the surrounding areas, Adam and Eve had blue eyes and long hair ... And we were all sons of Adam and Abraham! If the Bible said that the Good Lord had created Adam from the clay of the earth, how come he was white with blue eyes! Nobody said anything. Everyone seemed to be on board with the deal. An invisible hand then wrote messages, codes, and rules on the canvas of my soul in scarlet red letters that attached themselves there inside my brain, behind my head, dictating my place in this church, in Monbruno Court, in the city of Pointe-à-Pitre, in Guadeloupe, in the world . . . So, when I looked around me, when I saw all these people dancing, waltzing their way through their lives in this world, the image of this Good Lord that I had seen in the Church of Morne Massabiel came back to my mind. He was up on his pedestal and Jesus was still on his cross. And I and all the Guadeloupeans who passed back and forth at the feet of these statues, day after day, beating our chests like crabs and chanting it's-my-fault, we acquiesced. We accepted our fate as sons of Abraham and we accepted the curse of Ham! We were low-down, at his feet. Lower than his feet, even. Was that our rightful place?

I loved to read! I never belonged to the pink or green book club, a series of reading books for children, but I had read all the pages of the *Quelle* and *La Redoute* catalogs that Mom had glued together and pasted onto the metal sheets we used as walls in our two-room shack. I've never seen anyone do that kind of thing—making glue, mixing starch and water into a paste she called *lampois*. When I rediscovered the Bible, I was thrilled! The story of Genesis and Exodus and many of the other Old Testament books fascinated me. I spent hours and hours immersed in reading this book, imagining the interior of King David and Solomon's palace, questioning the mental health of Abraham when God asked him to sacrifice his firstborn son. The Children of Israel, the Philistines, and the life of Esther fascinated me and occupied my innocent childhood world. Around the age of fifteen, my friends and I discovered the Song of Songs. What a find! The boys had memorized many passages from this Biblical book, and they enjoyed reciting them to the girls. For their part, the girls were overjoyed, and they repeated the same verses aloud, especially when they knew that the object of their love could hear them:

Catholic Church

> Let him kiss me with the kisses of his mouth
> For your love is better than wine,
> Pleasing is the fragrance of your perfumes.
> Your name is perfume poured out
> No wonder the maidens love you!
> > (Song of Songs 1:2–3)

> His left hand is under my head,
> And his right arm embraces me!
> > (Song of Songs 2:6)

> Your navel is like a rounded bowl
> . . .
> Your two breasts are like two fauns.
> > (Song of Songs 7:2–3)

We were so shocked that this kind of language was included in the Bible that we decided to ask the elders of the Church for an explanation even though we enjoyed repeating these verses to ourselves over and over again.

"This book is a love letter from God to his Church" was the answer they gave us. And we shouldn't take everything literally. The problem for me was not simply the pornographic tone that these verses took. No! For us, it was clear that it was indeed the love between two beings who were attracted to each other and who were confessing their love. The text was beautiful, full of poetry. But vanity of vanities, explain to me the words of this lover:

> I am black, yet comely, O daughters of Jerusalem,
> Black like the tents of Kedar, like the tent curtains of Solomon.
> Do not stare at me because I am black,
> Because the sun burned my skin.
> > (Song of Songs 1:5–6)

95

And once again, an invisible hand was writing words on the lined pages of my soul, words that clung like iron claws, like talons from a bird of prey digging into the soft flesh of my consciousness. And the blood welled up, and the blood flowed . . . And I wondered . . .

I accepted the Lord at twelve years old. No one forced me. A simple invitation by my girlfriend who did not want to go to church alone changed my life forever. The evangelical church was just opposite Monbruno Court and right next to Carmont Court, and to my great astonishment, my mother had no problem letting me go with Madame Baduel who attended religiously every Wednesday and Sundays. Her daughter Josephat was bored to death at church and had asked me to come with her. For me, it was an opportunity to escape from my hole. My mother never let me go out, not even to stand for a moment in front of the entryway that led to our little shack at the very bottom of the street. So I lived like a crab that feared everything moving around in its universe. According to my mother, there were only dangers lying in wait for me out there, ready to rob me of my innocence!

I loved going to the evangelical church even though I only had one skirt and one blouse that my mother had hand-sewn for me. No need to say anything about the style. As always, that was all I had. However, while it's true that my friends at church never commented on my wardrobe, it's also true that I was constantly aware of my situation: poor and ugly but happy for a few hours to be somewhere other than under my mango tree and my tin roof.

To me, apart from the hymns we sang every Wednesday and every Sunday, and the Bible verses we memorized, and the messages we received from pastors and deacons (no deaconesses), the church was another like school, where I again felt like I was at the bottom of the ladder. It was a place where I learned that I was invisible. Sunday school and summer school classes didn't bring me anything, not even a tiny bit of hope. In the stories we were told,

Catholic Church

in the coloring books we had to color in without going outside the lines, there was never a question that these little boys or little girls were from another world, indeed from the same world that I was introduced to at the normal school through my French-language reading books. We were made to believe that all the Blacks of Monbruno Court, and all the Blacks of Guadeloupe, and perhaps even those of Martinique, this sister island of which I had heard, that we were the only souls who moved in this envelope of color. And that was a problem! Besides, in church did we not sing:

> Jesus by your precious blood
> You removed my iniquity!
> Look at me from up above
> tell me you pardoned me.
> I've wandered long with rebel heart,
> But hear your voice now calling me
> Confused and broken at your cross
> I now surrender totally.
>
> [Chorus 1]
> White, whiter than snow
> White, whiter than snow
> washed in the blood of the lamb
> I will be whiter than snow!

We were rebels, then, bearing on our skin the mark of our iniquity. Only the blood of Jesus could wash away our sins! Yes, whiter than snow. Hello?! That was our salvation! The snow!? Where would we find that in Guadeloupe? And how much would we need to save all Guadeloupeans? And God alone knew what rebels they were! I was listening, I was singing, my soul was still bleeding, and I was asking myself . . .

Well, our evangelical church was a place of purification. No more

97

CAMILLE'S LAKOU

Ka drums! That was the sound of evil! *Mizik a diab*—the Devil's music! No more carnival! That was just bacchanal and debauchery! No more braided hair! That was the mark of a woman's vanity, of someone who wanted to be noticed. Thank God, then, for the hot-comb to flat iron our hair and straighten it! I can still hear the noise the hot-comb made—pzzz!—when it came in contact with the skin on my ears. And the smell of my burning flesh. The experience always ended with small pink marks on my temples and ears. Whatever price I had to pay, though, it didn't matter because I *had* to have straight hair! My hair was so short that it stood up on my head after the hot-comb operation was done. I looked like a wet blackbird, but at least there weren't any peppercorn grains of hair on my head! And like they say, *zafè tchou mèl ki pran plon*—it ain't nobody's business but the bird whose ass is taking shots!

I remember the day when my cousin Maryse came to deliver me from this almost weekly torture. Because it must be admitted that the *négressité* of my hair returned with the slightest humidity in the air, from the least bit of rain, and of course after any shampooing. It was as if my own hair were rebelling against me, growing more and more bitter that the wide-toothed comb had so much trouble getting through. My deliverance from the sin of being a nappy-haired Black girl was a product called Byoliss that sat enthroned on the shelves of the Hibiscus supermarket in Raizet. A pretty young blonde with a sweetheart smile and lips the color of strawberries or raspberries decorated the front of the straightener box. There were boxes and boxes! I was sure they had enough for all of Guadeloupe! For all Guadeloupean women!

So I bought my box of Byoliss and my cousin applied the chemicals to my hair. The pain I felt on my young skull was more intense than the marks the hot-iron made on my ears. It mixed with the alkali smell coming off the jar of relaxer, stinging my eyes and making me cry out all the tears of my soul. But whatever! Freedom

Catholic Church

was finally within my reach. I was going to have hair like the white women! When Maryse finished rinsing the product, a lightness took hold of me in body and soul. My head felt lighter. My hair was falling on my forehead and also curling around my neck! My hair had grown longer! No more was it nappy. The teeth of the comb crossed back and forth over my skull without effort! What happiness! My hair was relaxed, relaxed! I shook my head back and forth and my hair followed the movement of my head! It was moving! I was going to be able to do like my long-haired girlfriends: sweep mine with the back of my hand while making a bobbing gesture with my head to make it settle in place behind my ears! Oh, the happiness that took hold of me that day! Oh, the joy of finally having silky hair! Unfortunately, my happiness was short-lived. A few days later, the same comb that glided smoothly over my skull now took with it clumps of hair! From the wet blackbird that I was after a hot-iron session, I had now become a dry-coconut head! And I wondered at what price . . . !

However, dry-coconut head or not, I continued to attend the evangelical church in Vieux-Bourg, Abymes, where I learned more life lessons. Among other things, I learned that it was not good for a woman to wear pants, since she was not a man; that as women we had to keep our mouths shut since we had nothing good to say. We were the cause of quarrels, nothing but the objects of fighting and discord. The primary duty of women: "As the church is subject to Christ, so wives must be subject to their husbands in all things" (Ephesians 5:24). "In all things!" I thought to myself, "Whoa, man, that's rough—*Woy mésyé! Bagay la bandé menm!*" On top of that, Paul told us in his Letter to the Corinthians, "Let women be silent in the assemblies, for it is not lawful for them to speak there. If they want to learn anything, let them ask their husbands at home; for it is improper for a woman to speak in church" (14:34).

So, not only was our situation as Black Guadeloupean women

CAMILLE'S LAKOU

dictated by the rules of outside authority, the Good Lord was also against us by relegating us women to subordinate status! So I will be the servant of my man and of my Lord! So be it! Amen. The neighborhood women said that if we were lucky, maybe we would find a man who would do something for us. These words, these observations all made their way along the same path in my mind. The messages followed, one after the other, and came to occupy this place in my memory where the secretary in charge of collecting information about my personality organized in extremely compart-mentalized categories all the codes, the messages, and any other important points that would form the person now known as Camille.

I heard, I saw, I listened, and I wondered . . .

My Crab Hole

Mon trou à crab

THE ALLEY PASSAGE that separated me from the street seemed endless. I hated it. As I said, without maternal permission, I did not have the right to cross it and go "out in the street." As a consequence, I often found myself doomed to sit in front of the door of our shack, watching the red and black ants hard at work transporting their food. I was fascinated by their discipline. They never stopped. Throughout their journey, they seemed to be exchanging messages without ever deviating from their path. They hardly ever mixed and mingled together, possibly never. The red ones that stung like hot peppers stayed with the red ones, the little black ones with the little black ones, the big biting ants with the big biting ants, and the order of things didn't seem to bother them at all. To my eyes, their mode of communication seemed identical: a quick kiss, then one went to the left and the other to the right while keeping the rhythm of things. Thus flowed the life of the ants. And it was like that. I never heard them quarrel. In fact, they were all following their destiny as ants. We Blacks, in Monbruno Court or elsewhere, we never flowed in the same direction. My mother always said we were like crabs in a barrel-*kon krab adan on bari!* I can still hear

CAMILLE'S LAKOU

it: "One keeps the other from escaping—*Yonn ka anpéché lot chapé lanmizè!*" So I learned early on that I could never count on my race to get me out of anything. So different from the life of ants!!

The alleyway in question was just a makeshift passage that had wedged itself between the house of Mr. Agapé, the neighborhood dog killer, and the garage of Uncle Rifa, my mother's older brother. There was barely room for an adult to get through with a moped. I remember my stepfather coming home every day after work with his yellow moped, Ti Jaune, pushing it almost in front of him, tripping over the pedal. It was pretty funny to think about it. I also remember the days when I persisted in learning how to ride a bike between the two walls of corrugated tin that framed this corridor. From my perspective as a child, it was so long that it seemed endless. I bumped sometimes on one side of the wall, sometimes on the other. Neither my stepfather nor my mother had ever volunteered to teach me how to stay up on a bike despite my tenacity to try again and again. Needless to say, I never managed to ride a bicycle there. Come to think of it, maybe my mother had found a way to make sure that I would never venture outside and frequent the little good-for-nothings of Monbruno Court as she called them!

Two openings served as windows and offered a gaping look into Monsieur Agapé's dark soul. This man lived alone in his house and carried on a mad love affair with the burning fire of sugar cane rum. His right hand stretched out and his fingers tightened around the neck of his favorite bottle of Karukéra rum. As if he were strangling it, he brought the bottle back to his mouth again and again. And Madame Karukéra relieved herself in his wide-open mouth, letting go of the stinking scent of all the pent-up misery inside Monsieur Agapé and the whole of Monbruno Court. He drank so much that his face puffed up as much as his belly and his lips sagged from kissing the weight of his miserable life. I never saw any women in the black hole that served as his abode. From time to time one of his

My Crab Hole

rumhead drinking buddies would visit him and sit with him, their eyes fixed on hopes of a tomorrow free from hunger. Sometimes a makeshift table was set up and there followed round after round of domino hands that went on endlessly until, of course, they abruptly stopped at the first sign of a well-sharpened knife.

Normal School

L'école normale

SO MY LITTLE FLOWER of life timidly raised its head toward the universe that surrounded me. All too soon, my younger cousins were gone, no more poop duets with my cousin Jean-Luc, no more vigils by the light of the single kerosene lamp, no more "krik krak" by Maryse. My stepfather would join us a few years later, but at that time it was only my mother and I, and I grew up under the shadow of the one character who sheltered my existence: the mango tree. During mango season, it would drop mangoes all day long that rolled across our tin rooftops and ended up in the narrow opening that separated our house from that of the Coquin family or in the canal that flowed all along the back of our little two-room shack. At night, these same mangoes that fell during the day took the form of blood-sucking *soukougnans* witches that used our house as a stopover. From up there, they decided what their next stop would be, perhaps at another house where they would settle accounts with some unfortunate negro who had bewitched his neighbor. So, they landed with all their weight on the roof and marched across the corrugated tin sheets with heavy, freewheeling footsteps, quickly taking flight to complete their task before dawn.

Normal School

I was afraid of *soukougnans*. Maryse had told me about them, and nothing could make me venture outside during those nights with or without moonlight. Luckily, my mother had taken great care to protect our shack with small crosses made of thorny acacia wood, which she had placed above each door. These thorns would certainly do a lot of harm to these witches and stop them from daring to enter our house. The outside noises and crackles were repeated throughout the night and kept me awake for a while not knowing if it was a mango that had fallen or the *soukougnans* indulging in their nightly dance parties on our roof. Bo! Bodo bo! Biblibliblibli ... Bep! I struggled to close my eyes, and my childhood imagination soon dragged me into a dream or nightmare where the mangoes rolling across the roof had *soukougnan* faces that little by little morphed into the face of a neighbor whose skin they were going to slip into and fly away flapping their wings. Bo! Bodo bo! I woke up again with a start!

Luckily, the morning came quickly. After bathing, and that session with my mother examining me to make sure I washed all the parts—the unmentionable ones along with all the others—I was ready to go to the normal school. I washed myself out of a small green plastic wash basin in which my mother had poured some very fresh water. First, I had to collect a little of this water with both hands, swish it around in my mouth and gargle well in the back of my throat, then spit it outside the little corner where we cooked. This first step was important and designed to bring your body to a certain temperature that aligned with the water in the basin. This was supposed to prevent you from catching a chill or perhaps dying from it. Mother had taught me to wash my face first, taking care to rub the corners of my eyes to get rid of all the crust that had formed during the night, then my nose where maybe a few insects had buried themselves overnight to become one with the boogersnot, and finally my mouth and the corner of the lips to remove all traces of any drool that had left a path winding down to my ears to prove I had slept on my back (which in general had to be avoided to prevent the soul from being stolen by evil spirits). Once the face was well washed, my arms and armpits came next before lowering myself into the basin so I could do a good job cleaning that part which could not be named. I finished with my feet, using the same water of course, but after all they were just feet. Whatever was left in the bowl was soon added to the canal water that passed behind our house and flowed away to join the wash basin water from other little girls and boys of the lakou.

After the morning wash ritual, my mother would give me my little lace dress that she had made for me herself. At first, I didn't mind. However, over the years, I became aware of the fact that I had to constantly adjust my dresses, especially at the neck level. For one reason or another, the neckline of my dresses was always crooked and kept strangling me, and the notches in my arms were never the same size. One side was a certain length, but the other side was either smaller or bigger. I had always thought that the problem came from the shape of my body. Later, at school, my classmates set about educating me on the root of my problem: my mother and her failed vocation as a seamstress! Yet my mother continued to make me wear her little creations and even ventured into teaching me how to sew. So I spent years wearing poorly cut clothes. Clean, but poorly cut. I still laugh at it, but even to this day I have an aversion to this mode of expression.

I was so happy when I got to join all the other little neighborhood kids on the road to the normal school. It was an opportunity for me to wear my little red and white plaid apron uniform with pockets on each side that I wore over a little white, short-sleeved knit sweater. It's true that mother made my own uniform, but this time she got help from Madame Baduel who showed her how to cut the fabric by following a pattern. For the shoes, as my feet kept growing,

Normal School

mother had made an opening in the end of the black patent leather uppers just to let my toes breathe, but they were now slowly escaping from the shoes, almost touching the ground at my feet. What surprised and later embarrassed me was when I realized that the other little girls were wearing pretty lace-up shoes that were never cut in front, and on top of that they had several pairs! The pair I was wearing was the same one I'd had for more than two years, and it hurt my toes. So many times, my mother had sent me to this man she claimed was my father so that I could ask him for a new pair of shoes. When I got to his house, he would always say, "Come back and see me next week." In the end, I insisted to my mother that she never send me back to this man who had no role other than that of being my biological father. Besides, I told her at the top of my six-year-old voice, she too had to stop counting on this man who had no interest in us and who obviously had no intention of doing anything for her! She recounted that he had never given her anything for me other than a jar of Nestle sweetened condensed milk and a baby bottle. That's all! I never understood what made her think that over the years he might change and give her something for me. Six years, and he had given me nothing! It wasn't like now he would suddenly do something for me!

The normal school was located at the foot of a hill that took a long time to climb. A little higher up, the road split in two with an artery that would reach the top of the hill where a teacher training institute was located and the canteen where the students ate during lunch time. The other small road went down toward the bottom of the hill to meet the primary school where I was going to spend the first years of my elementary school education. Arriving at the foot of the hill, we saw the main school and were impressed by its width. So, it opened wide its whitewashed façade to accommodate us in classrooms, boys downstairs and girls upstairs. The girls' recreation area was at the front of the building while the boys' was at the rear. That way, there was no risk of communication between the two sexes. Except in the case of Victor Rinaldo, a little boy our age whose mother had insisted that he be placed among the girls. After a few days when he seemed very uncomfortable to all of us, I think he suddenly realized that this was a big advantage for him since all the girls were running after him, including Christine Vialmolet, a blonde with hair as long as her legs. Her hair was so long that she had a hard time getting it done properly. Her hair was always so tangled and ruffled that we got the impression she never washed it. However, all the girls in the class had fun running their fingers through it, and brushing her hair like they did with their blue-eyed blonde dolls. This scenario, which was repeated almost every day during recess, was torture for me. I realized that all the girls in my class had much longer hair than mine. Every morning after my morning wash routine, I would sit on a small bench in front of my mother, who, sitting on a chair, would style my hair with a long-toothed comb. She soaked my head in bay rum, melissa balm water, and castor oil and then parted my hair with a line from my forehead to the bottom of my neck. She then grabbed my very short hair, forcefully twisted it into two small braids, one on each side of my head. She added to each braid a beautiful red ribbon much longer than the braid itself and I was then ready to go. I believe that all the girls in Monbruno Court and Popotte Court behind our house followed the same morning routine as me. I knew it was time for the morning hairstyle because I could hear the screams escaping from almost every house. On Saturday it was the cry of the pigs that were slaughtered for the Saturday night blood sausage and the Sunday meat, but every day we heard the cry of all the little girls who wailed because they were undergoing this hair ritual for little girl peppercorn hair that had to be domesticated, made to disappear, annihilated by hot iron or chemical to erase the Black, to deny the Black, to look more beautiful, more accepted, to succeed . . . I did not cry but I knew.

Normal School

I knew I had to somehow stifle everything in me that was Black if I hoped to get out of Monbruno Court one day. My classmates were luckier than me. They all came from very affluent families: they had lighter skin than I did, and they had long hair. There was Lise Angela with the big Italian eyes, Marie and Danielle Odhon with their mulatto hair, Brigitte Padasammy and her sister with the straight hair of "coolie Indians"—*zindien kouli*—and many others. I was pretty much the only one with short, nappy hair. Josephat Baduel, a little neighbor of my age who also lived in Monbruno Court, had much longer hair than mine and for one reason or another knew how to get out of a situation where she was made to feel inferior to others. Maybe because she had a mother and father who were married and living under one roof! That was not the case for me.

So once the hair comparisons were done, the girls took on Victor, who became their human doll on which they could do all sorts of experimentation. It even happened one day that all the girls in my class had agreed to take off his uniform pants to see what he had underneath. The teachers who were monitoring our recess arrived in time to rescue him. Poor thing, he probably still has nightmares! What an idea his mother had had to insist that he be placed with the girls. It's true that he looked very delicate and probably would have been devoured by the Black kids if he had attended the boys' school!

I still carry a rather fleeting memory of my early years in kindergarten, which was to the left of the big elementary school. I remember the first day my mother took me there. A lady had approached us and asked me to read her a few bits from a beautiful book with a shiny cover. I had never seen anything like it! I still remember its smell, which was different from the rancid smell of the Bible I was reading then. By the end of my reading, she had asked my mother a few questions and my mother replied by telling her that she had me read almost every day in her Bible, the only book we had in our shack. The lady immediately went to talk to another blond-haired girl who was apparently in charge of the whole school. Following this brief interview, my mother and her sister, who had also taken three of her children with them for the registration application, made their way back in great silence. Since that day, a chill had set in between the two. Grandmother apparently sided with Tante Carmelita, and my mother felt a veil, cold and wet like a dog's nose, wrap itself around her heart. Then Grandma's visits to our home became less and less frequent. We knew she was spending a lot of time with Tante Carmelita since they lived next door to each other, but the fact that she passed our little shack to go to Tante Amour's house made us very sad. From the conversations I was able to gather, it seems that they felt the school had taken into consideration the fact that mother had lighter skin than Carmelita, and they blamed her for that. I should say that, of all her family, for one reason or another, my mother had the lightest skin, almost like a *chabine*. That her mother never paid much attention to her, that her sisters hardly visited her, still seems to me today, with the distance caused by time, a great anomaly. Yet, whenever she could, my mother took me by the hand, and we both went to Tante Amour's house, to Tante Carmelita's house, which meant at the same time, to Grandma's house.

Out of my entire family, I was the only one admitted to the normal school that year. None of Tante Carmelita's children were accepted there. I never knew anything about it. So they all took the long walk to the school in the Sanitation district, which was much further away. The normal school was reputed to be the best in the area. It trained the teachers, and therefore benefitted from the best of the trainees. I do not know what this revealed about the other teachers in the few other schools in La Pointe!

I loved school, the books, the teachers. Madame Firmo was my favorite. She was very attentive to me since of all the other students in her class, I was the only one who could easily read the new words she put on the blackboard. She held me up as an example to all the

Normal School

other students and took me around to meet all the other teachers at recess. One day, she even took me home after class with another little student who, like me, already knew how to read. What an honor it was for me to be invited to my teacher's house! This visit sealed in me an even deeper love for school which became my getaway, a place where I could escape from Monbruno Court, which threatened at any moment to swallow me up in the routine that had taken over the lives of all those who lived there. Everything there seemed fine, but just like the pig who would always return to its mud bath and seemed to enjoy it, the men and women in the lakou seemed to have forgotten they had wings they could open to fly away. The lakou was their universe. And I wondered . . .

By inviting me to the small apartment where she lived in La Pointe, Madame Firmo led me to discover another type of life, one that was cleaner, more organized. The next day I received several side-eye glances from the other little girls who had heard of my visit to the teacher's house. From that day forward, I was quickly blacklisted. Their attitude became mocking, and no one dared to play with me during recess, so I was left alone just like in Monbruno Court. Alone again to create my own world, to observe the Black women who lived there, just as I used to observe the ants in my house and yard. And I continued to wonder . . .

Christmas was coming soon and for me it was a new source of joy. In Monbruno Court, Christmas meant music, pork, rice and *pwadibwa*, *siwo grozèy*, shrub, midnight masses and Oh-night-divine-when-Christ-was-born, and above all the time spent with family and neighbors. Throughout the year, my mom had saved all the peels from oranges we had eaten. She would take care to peel them well, starting from the top of the orange and forming a spiral that ended at the base. It was important not to break the skin before reaching the bottom of the orange. That would mean bad luck. She then had fun throwing the orange peel up in the air, hoping it would fall with the white side of the skin facing the sky. That would mean that the wish she had made while tossing the peel would soon come true. I never dared ask what her secret vow was. Year after year, our situation remained the same in Monbruno Court, and each season turned out the same, just like the previous one. If the white side of the skin was facing the sky, my mother was happy. If by contrast the yellow side was revealed, my mother's face would quickly darken. After that, she hurried to gather up the skin and put it outside to dry on a piece of sheet metal, exposed to the sun's rays. As Christmas approached, she would collect all her long-dried orange peels and soak them in a good liter of Damoiseau or Karukera rum. She added cinnamon, a nice, thick, black vanilla pod that she split in half lengthwise, a little grated nutmeg, and a tiny bit of sugar to kill the bitter taste of the orange rind. She let it all steep in a corner, well exposed to the heat of the sun. That way, her shrub drink could experience the natural warmth that, like a maternal kiss, added everything needed to sweeten this punch that carried in itself the flavor of Guadeloupe.

Once the shrub preparation was complete, mother turned to making sorrel syrup. I loved this syrup because it was red and sweet and because mother let me lick the pan. A few weeks before Christmas, she would go to the market and come back with her usual food, but also with hibiscus leaves of a certain variety that only bloomed toward the end of the year. She bought herself a good kilo and, once she got home, she cleaned them, separating the petals from the seeds so that she wouldn't have to worry about the petals. She let these petals soak in water that soon took on the blood-red color of the flower. After boiling the flowers, she collected this reddish water, which she boiled with enough sugar to obtain a light syrup that would go well with the local rum and become a house drink that was the delight of all the neighbors who would come to visit us without fail on Christmas Eve. After each sip, they would

Normal School

smack their lips to signify contentment and joy at being able to taste such a good syrup with such good rum. My own lips and my little six-year-old fingers had already given their approval. My way of enjoying it was to run my little fingers around the bottom and sides of the pan, lifting them to my lips again and again until the pan was very clean. I loved the sorrel syrup! I loved Christmas. I loved those moments that to me meant love of the country where we all lived, a country that loved us and gave us all these good things that made our hearts happy, and a country that we loved in return by celebrating our joy with all.

Shrub and sorrel syrup weren't the only drinks my mom made for Christmas. The most enjoyable for me was the coconut punch, and the whole process of *dlo pann* lasted for hours. I came to really admire my mother and the power she had in extracting this tasty milk out of the coconut. First, she had to rid the coconut of its outer shell. She often bought them well in advance and let them dry in a corner of the shack. Coconuts generally had smooth, green skin that soon turned a yellowish, slightly wrinkled color. Once they reached maturity, my mother would remove them from their thick layer of brown wood fibers that we call *pache*. The nut itself was well-nestled inside this thick coat of *pache*. To find it, you could simply split it in half with an ax while trying not to lose a hand in the process, or you could make a notch in the smooth skin and remove it with your hand or with a knife. Whichever method you chose, the nut soon revealed itself, like a treasure that refused to yield to your gluttony. This nut was hard as a rock, but we lusted after the fruit of its flesh. It was still well-hidden, though, and protected by two other trials: the shell and the fine membrane that covered the skin. My mother knew how to do it. She drilled two holes right into two of the three eyes that were already there in the nut. She let the water that came out collect in a glass and handed it to me, saying, "This'll refresh you." Next, she brought the nut to her lips while using a finger to plug up one of the holes she had just drilled. She blew very hard into the nut for several seconds and said this was to peel the flesh off the inside wall of the shell. After the blowing came the decasing time. She tapped hard and repeatedly all around the middle of the nut which revealed itself to us at the end, split in two. Then mother would take her knife and insert it between the shell and the flesh of the coconut to take it off the inner wall almost without difficulty. With this same sharp knife, she peeled the coconut to get rid of the thin, protective, light brown membrane. At this point, all that was left to be done was to collect all this pure white coconut flesh she was going to grate on the coconut grater. Woe unto me if I tried to help grate the coconut because with all those stroke, I always left a part of myself on the grater. That was not all! Once all the coconut was grated, mother took the pulp she had collected, put small quantities of it in a clean towel that she used only for this purpose. With only the force of her hands and wrists, she pressed, turned, and squeezed the pulp to extract the white milk that would serve as the basis for our tasty coconut punch. She added cream, vanilla, cinnamon and nutmeg plus a little lemon zest at the end. It all came together in this nectar that softened my childhood love of Christmas evenings. After giving me my portion, she added the rum that smelled like sugar cane. The scents of alcohol wafting off the coconut punch possessed my nostrils completely and imprinted in my consciousness the true flavor of my Guadeloupe.

Christmas Eve came, with its meals and culinary preparations that we only made once a year for this celebration. It was obvious that little Guadeloupe pigs *really* did not like the Saturday before Christmas. *Pwadibwa*, rice, and roasted pork were on the menu along with white yams. For us, this meal was almost sacred and bad luck was said to befall anyone who so much as touched the food before midnight Mass. Yet we ate these same pigeon peas throughout the months of November and December when they were in season.

Normal School

And the white yams were on my plate very often throughout the year with salted cod and Alba oil. "What's so different about this meal?" I asked my mother one day. "Well," she replied, "Christmas is the day of the Christ child, the Virgin Mary, and Joseph. We have to go to church first to see Baby Jesus in the crèche and after listening to the priest, we go home and then we can eat meat." I was very perplexed by this answer, which did nothing to enlighten me. Still, I understood that no one should eat before going to midnight Mass. Needless to say, we children were dying of hunger leading up to Mass. Not a single tiny morsel of bread was to cross our lips before Mass, but I could make neither heads nor tails of this rule. How could a little white baby, in fact, a doll with blue eyes that was placed on a small pile of straw, between two other statues that were said to be its parents, and surrounded by animals, have so much power over Guadeloupeans that it was able to dictate the time of our Christmas meal? Fortunately, there were Christmas carols. From the beginning of the month, M. Couchy entertained us with his Christmas hit parade and prepared us for the advent of Baby Jesus:

> Joseph, my faithful dear
> Let us look for housing
> Time is short and childbirth is calling me
> I feel the fruit of life
> This dear child of heaven
> Whose holy life will appear before our eyes

This was followed by:

> Michaud was watching, Michaud was watching
> At night in his thatched cottage,
> Near the hamlet, near the hamlet
> Keeping his flock
> The sky was shining, the sky was shining

With a living light
Then he began to sing
"I see, I see the shepherd's star" (repeat)

Then it was:

In the quiet of the night
A mighty noise was heard
One voice, a host of voices
Angelic more than human
One voice, a host of voices
Singing glory to the king of kings.

And finally:

He is born, the holy child
Play oboe, let bagpipes ring

These songs instilled very strong messages in us and prepared us for the adoration of our new king. They reminded us of the miserable lives of his parents who, just like us, owned nothing, were poor and homeless. They also summoned us to wake up and pay homage to our soon-to-be-born Savior. For me, other than the fact that I starved every Christmas Eve, I had a hard time understanding the relationship between Baby Jesus and me and mine. We never talked about him at home, but suddenly in December, even though he wasn't even born yet, he was already in control of our stomachs! Of course, I loved the songs and all the preparations that heralded the coming of the Christ child, but I still could never figure out what he was bringing to us since the year that was over hadn't changed in any way from the one that had preceded it.

This is how Christmas and its rum and its different punches flowed. Families got together to share meals together. Little Jesus

Normal School

gave us permission to eat by the advent of his birth and everyone was in a hurry to leave the church to eat what was waiting for us. I had already dozed off so many times on the lap of my mother who was rushing me to wake up so she could take us home.

I only had to wait until Sunday after Christmas for the Mass of the Innocents, another celebration that would potentially bring a little joy to my heart. On this day, all the children in the neighborhood went to Mass with the toys that Santa had brought them. So, he was different from Baby Jesus. I had met him at the normal school. In fact, word had it that he was the one who brought us toys when we were smart. Actually, one time, it wasn't until a day or two after our mistresses had told us about the arrival of Santa Claus that Santa came to see us.

We had all been brought to the playground and our parents had dressed us in our Sunday clothes. For me, it was a simple little pink dress with lace that extended below and a little white lace apron that I wore over it. One of my mother's creations, and I was very proud of it at the time. I also wore my pretty Sunday shoes that my mother had to cut at the toes since they were now too small for me and squeezing my constantly growing feet. She kept reproaching me about that, by the way, and reminding me that I certainly had my father's feet since hers were so small.

On the lawn, which was adorned with golden garlands and balloons of all colors, we were all so eager to see Santa Claus arrive. The atmosphere was so thick with excitement that we could have cut it with a machete! And for me, who didn't have a father at home, I was boiling inside at the thought of meeting this father figure who was giving out toys to the children with such kindness and charity. According to my schoolbook reading, he usually arrived in the evening and came in through the fireplace to drop off toys at the foot of the tree. As a matter of fact, he never stopped in front of the crèche. I actually think that there was discord between him and the Baby

Jesus, who first woke us up in the middle of the night and had to receive the gifts that the kings brought him before he let us eat our Christmas meal. Santa, at least, came straight to us with all the toys. All we had to do was stay nice all year. So I didn't need to dwell on small details like the lack of a fireplace in the Monbruno Court. In fact, I never saw one anywhere we went in La Pointe! Not a single chimney in sight! How would he get in? He would certainly get hurt while trying to make a hole in our tin roofs! Also, he came when it was cold and when it was snowing. Snow had never fallen in the Monbruno lakou as far as I know. Another thing I tried not to think about was Santa's outfit. According to the pictures in our reading book, he always wore a long robe that was thick and red, with white fur lining, and he wore a hat, the tip of which fell down his back, almost touching the bag he carried on his back. According to what we were told, this sack contained the toys for all the children of the Monbruno Court and the adjoining communes. I had my doubts about this distribution of gifts, but I was consoled by telling myself that I had been nice and I knew who around me was not. I kept a close eye on Charlot, who had said some swear words to me and even tried to touch my behind. I was sure he would not receive any gifts. So maybe this sack, which didn't even exist in our universe, must have been magical.

The schoolteachers had put us in a circle and made us sing Christmas songs that were very different from our Monbruno Court hymns. Among them were:

> Little Father Christmas
> When you come down from heaven
> With toys by the thousands
> Don't forget my little shoes
> . . .
> I can't wait for daybreak
> To see if you brought me

Normal School

All the beautiful toys I see in my dreams
And that I asked you to bring

And then again:

On the long road
All white with white snow
A nice old man is coming
With his cane in his hand
And way up high the wind
That whistles through the branches
Gives breath to the romance
He sang when he was a child:

Long live the wind, the wind
Long live the winter wind
That goes whistling, blowing
In the big green fir trees . . .
Oh! Long live the season
Long live the winter season
Snowballs and New Year's Day
And Happy New Year, grandma . . .

And also:

My beautiful fir tree, king of the forests
How I love your greenery
When in winter, woods and fields
Are stripped of all their charms
My beautiful fir tree, king of the forests
You keep all your adornment

Suddenly, a commotion rose up in the schoolyard with shouts of "There he is!" and "He's here!" But even though I was looking everywhere with my two little *moun lakou* eyes, I couldn't see anything,

119

I couldn't see anyone. A teacher yelled, "He's on the roof! Look at his sleigh!" Another said, "He's already gone, he's passed over the roof of the bathrooms!" What a shame, I missed it too. And the teachers immediately directed us to our respective classrooms. Oh my God! Dolls, little white dolls with beautiful smooth hair that our fingers could pass through without getting stuck! Ah, if I had hair like that! Each little girl had on her desk a little white doll with very pink cheeks and blue eyes that pierced your soul! The boys had cars and with that, they were over the moon! Cars! What were we learning from that? We girls, we were at the height of happiness, and me more than everybody else! Imagine that up to then, I had never received any gifts, not even for my birthday. So I was almost dizzy with so much happiness in my heart and so much joy around me. For a little girl whose daily life included only a mango tree surrounded by wooden shacks with tin roofs, the school offered a universe whose horizon stretched beyond her imagination. This doll symbolized another world, made palpable through the pages of these books that smelled so good of faraway lands, impossible worlds, but that was at the same time a world where no one had any problems.

So, at the normal school, Christmas had a different meaning. At first it was the snow, the cold, the houses buried in the snow as if wrapped in an all-white coat, the chimneys, the wood that had to be cut to feed the fireplace, the turkey stuffed with chestnuts that would be eaten with gusto on Christmas Eve by a family that consisted of father and mother whose two children were a girl and a boy. No neighbors, no grandmas, no cousins. A strange Christmas that one aspired to because it came from books. Thus was born in me the phenomenon of a double personality—one that I wore at the normal school and the other that was revealed once I took off my French cloak and, along with it, the things that I needed to learn and practice to one day become a proper woman.

Normal School

After Christmas would come Carnival and Mardi Gras, which would give Guadeloupeans permission to roam the streets from January to February. From the first Sunday in January, the first groups of masquerade bands began to parade through the streets to the tumultuous musical sounds that generally accompanied the road marches and performances. I could hear them coming from far away, and their approach created a panic in me that was paralyzing. *Mas a konn* captured the indomitable force of the bull; in *mas a goudron* or *mas a congo* the entire body was coated with blackened molasses and lips were reddened with *roucou* paste to represent the African origin of Caribbean Blacks. *Mas a lanmo* troupes were draped in long white shrouds lined with small needles in which they wrapped you up if you had the misfortune to be in their way. They represented the death that awaited you at all times. The *mas a fwèt* players all carried long whips that they cracked incessantly in the air. They no doubt represented the whip of the master who knew so well how to caress the backs of Black people. The children of the neighborhood all fled their approach. I have never been so happy as I was with the knowledge that between all those masks and me was that long corridor that separated our little shack from the gate that opened onto Monbruno Court. The *mas a riban* were the least frightening. I've only seen them once but I still remember them very well. They all wore very colorful clothes, and each held in their hand a long ribbon of a different color, the other end of which was hung on a very high pole, a kind of mast, which they held as if it were planted in the ground. They danced in a circle to the sound of the music while intertwining around the mast in a very colorful way. They reminded us of the Indian presence on the island. They didn't scare me.

I had caught the sound of the drum from a great distance, probably as far away as Broucard Court. They were on their way to Monbruno. My whole body was beginning to vibrate. My mother was

CAMILLE'S LAKOU

watching me, and she didn't seem to be worried. There was even little smile playing on the corner of her lips that did nothing to reassure me. I lived every Sunday during carnival season like this, caught between the fear of being chased by demonic masqueraders but also a frenzy that grabbed me in the gut whenever I heard the sound of the drum that accompanied the masked dancers. It started in my stomach and made me tremble all over, because the Ka drum knew how to speak to me, reassure me, and bring me joy even in the midst of fear.

> Oh, what a beautiful month is March, . . .
> The stream is no longer frozen.
> the earth is no longer hard.
> (Alfred de Musset)

My books told me to be on the lookout for springtime in March. It was coming with rains, budding plants, peaches, apples, and pears. Squirrels and deer would soon begin to roam the land, having shed their heavy coats that shielded them from the cold and the snow. The rich, abundant earth would give birth to thousands of new lives, and the birds would begin to sing again.

Around me, in Monbruno Court, the same mango tree was pounding our corrugated tin roofs, dropping mango bombs that would keep falling, rolling, jumping, and then bursting open on either side above our two-room shack. Or else they would get stuck on the roof and rot there, perfuming the rainwater we would collect during rainy season to fill the barrels with, to keep from having to go back and forth to the fountain. No unfrozen streams, no budding flowers, no strawberries or raspberries. In fact, I realized that even birds avoided our neighborhood. The few trees that cut through the monotony of the courtyard were a refuge only for bats that came out in the late afternoon.

Normal School

Yet I knew that the mango tree under which I grew up and those wandering Guadeloupean souls around me were all, in one way or another, a part of myself. I couldn't explain it, but I knew that I could not be something other than this little Black girl with the nappy hair from Monbruno Court. I was bound to this environment, to these people, to these noises, to these tastes, to these smells! And that was everything that made me the little girl I was, watching everyone around her and collecting all the different messages to safeguard them in her mind. These messages were what would, over the years, without my even having to think about it, dictate to me my place, my behavior, my reflections, and my reaction to the world around me.

Conclusion

Manor's Alley

THE TELEPHONE RANG. In general, when it was the landline, that meant a call coming in from overseas. Evelyn hurried to pick it up.

"Good Morning! Achieve with Camille! How can I help you?"

At the sound of the voice coming from the other end of the line, Evelyn froze. Her face turned a shade of terra cotta and the blood drained from her cheeks. Her entire body began to tremble. From her personal office across the room, Camille could see all that was happening in Evelyn's little office space.

"*Kay rivé*, Evelyn? What's going on?"

"It's my mother," she muttered in a tone of total despair. She turned her back to Camille and started a conversation with her mother. Right away, Camille heard little cries being stifled, and she looked up to see Evelyn collapse in her chair. When she saw her shoulders shaking, Camille knew that Evelyn was crying, so she waited until the call had ended.

Evelyn put the telephone down and remained with her back turned, her gaze fixed on the big bay window that looked onto Jean-Luc's tropical garden. Outside, it was raining and the dark sky reflected Evelyn's state of mind. She was now crying softly and tears were running down her cheeks. She made no effort to dry them. Three years of never setting foot in her country! Three years of giving her parents excuse after excuse about not going back to Jamaica in order to avoid admitting her shame and having it revealed. Her son was now five years old! Two years after starting at the Chamberlains, she had gone back very briefly when her grandmother

127

died, but she never found the courage then to admit to them that she had a two-year-old son. And now her father was surely going to die. Her mother was calling to tell her that he was much worse and the doctors did not know how much time he had left to live. What would she do? How would she explain her situation to them? Above all, she would not want to run the risk of aggravating her father's condition. She would never forgive herself for that!

She got up from her chair and walked shakily toward Camille who watched her from a distance.

"Mrs. Chamberlain, I need to talk to you. I need help! I'm going crazy!"

"What's wrong Evelyn? You know very well you are like a daughter to us. What can we do for you?"

"*Papa mwen malad*. Mi fadda sick. I have to go home."

"Ok, no problem! Take as much time as you need. Are you taking little Marvel with you? You know you can leave him with us if you want."

Evelyn let out a sigh of despair.

"What," Camille asked in an incredulous tone, "you never said anything to your parents? You talk to your mother every Sunday!"

"Mi no av di courage, Mrs. Camille. I tried many times but I just could not bring myself to do it. In fact, I didn't want to face this situation. I could never have the strength to look Papa in the face and admit all that I've done."

"Well, Evelyn dearest," Camille replied in English, "listen to me! It's not a mistake . . . Your life is not a mistake! Marvel is not a mistake! Yes, the events of his arrival were quite traumatic for you. This is a part of your life circumstances. We all understand that, and I know we could never feel what you felt through it all. However, your life circumstances are not who you, Evelyn, are. You're more than that and you must remember that your parents love you no matter what, just like you love little Marvel. *Fanm tonbé pa*

Manor's Alley

jenmen dézespéré, my girl, a woman falls, but she never despairs.

"Look at yourself!" Camille continued in French. "Look at your child! How could you deny how lucky you are to have been chosen by the universe to be his mother! Charly was nothing more than an instrument . . . Well, let's not even talk about him now!"

Evelyn stopped her abruptly and fixed her eyes on Camille like a little lost dog. She had a somber look of deep, palpable pain. Her beautiful almond-shaped eyes were puffy and swollen, and her eyelids had taken on a bruised purplish color that clashed with her ebony tint.

"How could I explain to my parents that I have a five-year-old son who they don't even know exists? And the neighbors? Yaad people nah forgive! And my father? I do not want to be the final nail in his coffin. I can't even bear the thought of that. I have to be on the next flight to Kingston. Oh my God, Jesus, and the Virgin Mary!"

With one firm hand, Camille gripped Evelyn by the shoulder. With the other, she lifted up her face where the mascara Evelyn had applied so carefully that morning was now smeared and running (she never faced the world without first fixing her makeup with great care).

"Listen to me, Evelyn. You have been here with me for the past five years, right?"

"Yes, Mrs. Camille," she said while sniffling loudly.

"You've accompanied me on many of my trips to Africa, Haiti, and France, right? I've even told you the story of my childhood and all the things that have brought me here, to this very house where you have raised little Marvel."

"And I'm grateful, Mrs. Camille. You and Jean-Luc are like parents to me. I could never thank you enough. And . . ."

"What I'm getting at, Evelyn," Camille interrupted, "is that, whether we like it or not, we are the masters of our own destiny. Our decisions are not taken by chance. And if you are here where

129

you are now, that is because of the choices you made in your life, in the past. Deliberately or not, the things that you stored in your subconscious have formed the person that you are now."

At these words Evelyn looked up, ready to retaliate. She was certainly not about to let Camille reproach her for anything. She had not *chosen* to have a baby at seventeen, and above all not with a good-for-nothing like Charly. Sure, good luck had put this family in her path, and they worried about her and helped her raise her child, all while continuing her studies. Thanks to their support, she had graduated magna cum laude from UCF. She reminded herself that she had had to concoct another story to keep her parents from coming to see her receive her diploma. They were so proud of her, and so disappointed at not being able to be there for graduation. Thanks to the Chamberlains—as always—she was ready to start her MBA the very next semester and little Marvel attended one of the best schools in Orlando. It was true that she had many reasons to be grateful. But despite all these years working for the Chamberlains, she could not stop herself from being a little skeptical, and even a lot skeptical. Yet and still, had she not seen how many lives had changed thanks to Camille's program? She never let herself get involved. She did her job, scheduled meetings, accompanied Camille to her international conferences when Jean-Luc was too busy at the restaurant, made sure the website was maintained, kept up the blog, organized the numerous workshops that Camille directed, et cetera. But to let herself believe all of that nonsense? That was another story! At any rate, Camille had stopped trying to convince her.

Evelyn open and closed her mouth several times trying to respond to Camille's remarks. She couldn't do anything except sit back and continue to listen. What good would it do to contradict Camille?

So Camille went on:

"I know that you don't think much of all these stories about meditation, EFT, positivity, living in the moment, and so on. But it won't

Manor's Alley

cost you anything to listen to me now. You believe in the Bible, right? I know you do because there is a really big one on your nightstand."

Evelyn just shrugged her shoulders without saying anything.

"Well, the Bible says: 'Do not worry about tomorrow, because tomorrow will worry about itself. Sufficient unto the day is the evil thereof' (Matthew 6:34). You know what that means? It means we only have the present moment. Now, this moment that we are living in, right here, you and me. Forget yesterday. Tomorrow does not exist, and it will never exist, my dear, so live this moment intensely. The fear you have about offending your parents is vain. They are not here now. Look around you. What do you see? Go ahead, tell me, what do you see?"

Evelyn heaved a great sigh, raised her eyes and began:

"I see you, I see your desk, I see my desk, I see outside through the pretty circular bay window. I see Jean-Luc's garden, I see that the rain has stopped falling. I see Jean-Luc playing with Marvel close to the lake . . ." She felt her heart melting.

She took her head in her hands and continued: "I see . . ."

"So that," said Camille, "is your Now. That is your life. It is all that we have, now, here, you and me. Do you have a problem with what you see now?"

She shook her head, "No!"

"Accept this moment and cherish it. Life, my dear, is nothing but a series of Nows. Live each of them intensely. If you try to give the best of yourself to each moment, you live your best life. Tomorrow is a liar that will continue to make false promises. So don't worry yourself about your parents' reaction. When the time comes, you will know what to do. Go make some reservations, then. Book four tickets because we're coming with you, and little Marvel is going to make his first trip to Jamaica! Things could not have turned out better than this. We'll leave for the conference in Guadeloupe directly from Jamaica and we will all make this trip together if possible. The universe does its work very well. Nothing is left to chance."

Camille gave all these orders without even looking at Evelyn, who could only shrug her shoulders and shake her head. She knew that the Chamberlains would support her in whatever way she needed.

Jean-Luc and Marvel came in from the garden. Marvel ran to his mother, crying, "Mommy, mommy! When are we going to Jamaica? Jean-Luc told me they have the best patties there. Mom-meeee, tell me when are we going? I want to go there and eat beef patties all day long!"

Evelyn squatted down there and opened her arms wide to scoop up little Marvel, who buried his head in her bosom, all the while laughing. His locks covered his forehead and the nape of his neck too. He smelled good from the fresh air outside after the rain. His locks were full of the scent of orange blossoms, and Evelyn's heart cracked open with love for this child. How handsome this boy was! He brought so much happiness to her heart. Had the universe been meddling in her business after all? She had not spoken of Jamaica to little Marvel in months! Was that a sign? She raised her head and looked at Camille, who was herself enlaced in the arms of Jean-Luc. He kissed her gently on the neck and Evelyn thought, Those two will never tire of each other.

"I'm going to take a nice hot shower," said Jean-Luc. "What do you want to eat tonight, Camille? I think I have everything we need to make a good pizza! Evelyn, tell Madame Ezéchiel to heat up the pizza oven. Thank you, my girl!" With those words, he left Camille and headed toward the bathroom that took up the entire southern wing of their Florida villa.

Camille tossed a look at Evelyn and shrugged her shoulders. She sat up, buried her head in the computer screen, and continued to revise the last lines of her novel, entitled *Moun Lakou*!

TRANSLATED IN ORLANDO, SAINT KITTS, COLUMBIA, NEVIS, AND GUADELOUPE, 2018–2024